FINAL PRICE

J. GREGORY SMITH

PUBLISHED BY
amazon encore

The characters and events portrayed in this book are fictitious. Any similarity to real persons, living or dead, is coincidental and not intended by the author.

Printed in the United States of America

Published by AmazonEncore
P.O. Box 400818
Las Vegas, NV 89140

ISBN-13: 9781935597186
ISBN-10: 1935597183

For Julie,
who always believed in me.

ACKNOWLEDGEMENTS

I want to thank all the readers and professionals who endured the early drafts and provided invaluable feedback and editorial advice, especially Connie G-B.

Thanks to Justynn Tyme for the terrific cover design of the independent edition.

Thank you to the team at AmazonEncore for giving me this opportunity and for all the work to get the book ready as well as spreading the word.

Thanks to my family for their infinite patience and understanding.

Last but not least, thanks to Jeff B. for the "research" opportunity.

PROLOGUE

Elsmere, Delaware (just outside of Wilmington)

Sweat and condensation ran down the inside of the rubber Gandhi mask, but he wasn't ready to take it off. He locked the door to Nguyen's Oriental Grocery and spun the sign to read "Closed."

He giggled and skipped through the store. Aisles of canned goods sat next to fresh produce and bins of iced seafood. Fish odors mingled with ginger. He heard muffled sounds from the back room. Not loud enough to reach the street, just enough for him to enjoy.

He returned to the storeroom where he had stashed the owners. Ms. Min and Mr. Tran remained tied to chairs. The duct tape he slapped over their lying mouths held fast, more than a match for their sweaty little faces. Best of all, he savored the shine of fear in their eyes. Fabulous. Why hadn't he tried this a long time ago?

Showtime. He squatted in front of the husband, Tran, and waggled the pistol. He held up a thin wad of bills and rubbed the insulting pittance from the cash register under Tran's nose.

"Where's the rest?"

The Vietnamese man shook his head.

He tore the tape off Tran's mouth, then Min's.

"Tell me."

"No rest," Tran said.

Who's in charge here? He stood in front of the slight woman and slid the barrel of the gun along her cheek and into her mouth like it was part of him. So good. His masked head lolled back, and he let out a sigh. She yelped around the cold steel.

"Okay! I tell you!" Tran said.

He listened, found a hidden box, and removed a large roll of bills.

"That's better." He walked out into the store, picked up a basket, and filled it with groceries. Blood pounded through his body, and he struggled to keep his breathing even to show icy control. Ready now.

He stood in front of the couple and pulled off the rubber mask. Cool air. Their eyes opened wide, but they said nothing. It was a start.

"Good. I was worried we all looked alike to you. This," he said as he held the money box contents, "is for all my time and sweat last week. We had a deal, but I see you bought from Marlo."

He leaned in toward Min and affected an Asian accent. "You get good price, riiiight?"

Min remained silent. Her jaw clenched, and those dark eyes locked him out.

"Tell your husband why you cancelled the deal. What did you say to me?" She shook her head.

Stubborn little… "Say it. What about the interest rate? What did you say?" His grip tightened on the gun.

"Too high." Sounded like a puff of wind. He made her repeat. Musical this time.

He reached into the basket and held up a can of bamboo shoots.

"How much?"

"Take, you take please."

"No. How much? How much for this?"

"One—one dollar seventy-nine cents."

"Tooo high." He mimicked her and dropped the can in her lap.

He turned to Tran and held up a head of lettuce. "How much?"

"Dollar ninety-five."

"Tooo high." He continued until the basket was empty. He pressed the gun into their necks when they tried to beg.

"Now, be quiet while I leave." He re-taped their mouths.

He stepped behind Tran and picked up a ripe melon. He jammed it over the barrel of the Ruger .22 pistol. Min saw and tried to scream. She made muffled noises along with the muted pops when he fired into the back of Tran's head. Only the pulp marked where the tiny slugs entered. Where was the blood? Tran's head shook and his body twitched.

There! Blood and melon juice ran down Tran's neck. Tran shuddered once more and was still. Min thrashed and her throat bulged with smothered screams. He gripped the back of her chair to steady it. She stopped moving and tears slid down her face.

He leaned over and whispered in Min's ear, like a lover. "Tooo high." He took more care with his aim and shot her twice in the base of her skull, the way he used to finish off alley cats as a kid.

Just as well. He knew she wasn't up to being a widow.

CHAPTER 1

No Place Like Home

Newark, Delaware

It was two o'clock in the morning, and Paul Chang knew his mother would get out of bed before long. Her caregiver, Shu, opened the door the instant Chang rapped on the thick wood. He might sleep even less than Chang.

"Good morning, Master Paul." Shu made a deep bow. He looked thinner and balder than ever.

"Hello, Shu." Chang returned the bow, and his back muscles howled. Long shifts in the cruiser made him feel brittle. Too much target practice and not enough stretching. He never should have stopped his training with Shu.

"What have I told you about opening the door to anyone without checking?"

"I only open for you, Master Paul."

"But I could have been a bad person, understand?"

The old man smiled. Why did he waste his breath?

"You have good heart, no matter what anyone say." Shu nodded to the stairs. "She will be awake soon."

"Let's get started."

* * *

"Too much." Chang winced at the old man's tug. Shu always forced Chang's legs until he thought the tendons would tear.

"Keep anger in muscles, no room for stretch." Shu pulled again.

"It's the job." Chang braced for the stick. Shu struck him on the shoulders with his shattered bamboo practice sword.

"Man who keep eyes closed, always blind. Anger from here." Shu rapped the side of Chang's head.

He tried not to provoke Shu for the rest of the workout, and the tightness between his shoulders eased. Time to get back to work soon; he might escape Mother tonight after all.

The intercom in the basement crackled, and his mother's voice shattered the peace.

"Shuuuuu!"

* * *

Chang mounted the stairs and allowed his gaze to pass over the ancient treasures. The silk prints alone were worth more than the house. They belonged in a museum, but Mother was deaf to the suggestion.

He forced himself to walk the few feet to the bedroom door where his mother waited. He knocked. No answer. He smelled sandalwood from the incense cones she burned night and day.

"Mother?" he called out in Mandarin. "It's Paul. Are you there?"

"Where else? Open it." Her sharp voice cut through the panels. She spoke English with a heavy accent. Chang took a deep breath and turned the knob.

The tiny woman perched in her large bed in a bright blue silk bathrobe embroidered with a print of a tiger and a dragon locked in combat. She wore her hair pulled back in a bun as usual, and though she had wrinkles around her eyes, Chang still didn't see much gray. Gray on the inside.

"You sound American. So speak American."

He switched back to English. "I thought it might be nice to practice."

"Why bother?"

"How are you feeling?"

"Why you wait so long to see me?"

More broken links in the chain of her mind.

"I was here last week."

"You have so much time? Why you not work now?"

"It's the middle of the night for everyone else but you, Mother. Even bad people need to sleep." The graveyard shift was just fine with him. Fewer people to deal with, and he couldn't sleep anyway.

"Why you get such bad times? You going to get fired, like in New York?"

"I wasn't fired. I left the force, and they helped me start over in Delaware. Everyone agreed it was for the best." Better than jail, but that didn't concern her.

The same questions every time. Each visit the scorn played out like a video loop. The old woman rolled back Chang's forty years, shrank his six-four height, and turned him into a little kid again.

She made him think about how after his first growth spurt the other Chinese kids reveled in playing "Chase the

Water Buffalo." He didn't know how to defend himself then, and a short kid would bait him. When he tried to retaliate, other kids jumped him from behind. If he ran, they chased him like a pack of animals. Eventually he'd fall down, usually in an alley, exhausted and unable to fight back.

When he limped home, covered in cuts and bruises, his mother told him his cowardice shamed the family. For years he believed her.

"You bring shame to police like you bring to family."

"Please, Mother. Not tonight. I found Uncle Tuen's killer, gave him justice. I *know* you remember."

She could remember that and more.

"Make your father sell business. Not take over like good son. Have to try to change past. Tuen gone, but we still alive. Business still alive, but you fight gang. Make us run here, lose face." Her dark eyes burned.

She hit his weak points like a Shaolin master.

"You believe in destiny, Mother. Why can't you accept that?"

"Same destiny make you marry cat-face white girl?"

Not for long. Colleen never developed the calluses. Chang ignored a flare of pain in his stomach. He liked to play with the lie that Mother alone drove her off.

"Colleen moved away." He was tired, but sleep didn't always refresh.

"You smell American."

"Is Shu making you take your medicine?"

"Medicine don't work. I tell Shu he fired. He never listen. You never listen either. Maybe you get it from me." If she smiled, she might have done so now.

Chang's pager began to beep. He glanced at the code. Homicide.

"Mother, I have to answer this, but I'll see you next week." Good excuse to leave.

CHAPTER 2
Pulp

Chang eased the blue Crown Victoria into the handicapped spot outside the 7-Eleven off Union Street in Wilmington.

Compared to New York, murders in Delaware came at a more manageable pace. Until lately. He opened the door to the cruiser and grabbed his camera.

Chang stepped under the yellow police tape and ignored the looks that said, "Biggest Chinaman I ever saw!" A Wilmington PD officer greeted Chang. Young, barely over twenty-one. Teeth could have been bleached. The nameplate read "Scott Gilpin."

"Detective Chang? Glad you could get here so fast."

Chang was used to being recognized in this state that was more like an overgrown small town. It didn't hurt that he was the only Asian-American officer in the homicide department of the state police.

"What have we got?" Chang looked around the store. A pair of sandaled feet stuck out from behind the counter. The smell of overcooked coffee hung in the air along with hot dogs and that distinctive coppery odor.

"We got a 911 call from a guy who came in for coffee and found the body. I responded and, well, see for yourself." Gilpin wore an ashen look that told Chang he'd handled more parking tickets than corpses.

Chang peered over the counter, and a whiff of citrus caught his attention. Indian male victim, no more than five-six and 140 pounds. Chang saw what appeared to be two gunshot wounds to the face, probably a pistol. Small entry holes and at least one larger exit wound. Chang's pulse jumped when he saw what accompanied the bullet holes.

A lemon lay smashed across the victim's face, the fragrant juice mingled with congealed blood. Chang began his photo series.

"You ever see anything like this in New York, sir?"

"No. Is the money gone from the register?" Chang continued to move around the counter and photographed different angles of the body. He kept his breathing slow despite his rapid heartbeat.

"Yeah, till's cleaned out, so I figured robbery, but then I saw that lemon and it didn't fit."

"Videotape?"

"Be right back." Gilpin headed towards the back room.

"I'll go with you. Our guy had to be in a hurry, especially if he took the time to do that with the lemon." The fruit did not smell rotten. What the killer did took force.

In the back room, stacks of cups and other supplies littered the floor. Chang found the video recorder for the security cameras. He took one look and saw the tape was gone. Clearheaded act. Premeditated murder?

"Gilpin."

"Yes, sir?"

"See if you can find the videotape. Check the nearby dumpsters. Maybe we'll get lucky."

"I'll look around, sir."

Chang knew state troopers didn't normally order other departments to "dumpster dive," but Gilpin looked bright enough to recognize what a key piece of evidence in a homicide case might mean to his career.

Chang walked over to a second city police cruiser. Time to get a statement from the civilian who found the body. An Officer Burris stood guard. He was almost as tall as Chang and carried a roll of weight around the middle.

Burris glanced at Chang's identification. "Oh good, the cavalry. I feel so much safer now that a professional is here." He shifted his gaze to Chang's neck. His scar. "You lose a sword fight or something?"

Chang felt blood rise in his face. He didn't know if the witness could hear Burris inside the car or not. He stepped close enough to smell garlic.

"I didn't lose. Does this man have a name?"

Burris stepped back and shoved a clipboard at Chang. "You're the expert—it's all here."

Chang scanned the report. The man in the cruiser, Norm Chandler, found the victim, Rami Patel, shot dead. Patel, thirty-six, no wife, no kids. Chang stared at Burris until he moved away, then opened the car door.

"Mr. Chandler?" The man looked up. He appeared to be in his early fifties. Chang introduced himself. "I understand you were the first to find the deceased?"

"I guess so. I called it in as soon as I saw what happened."

"Tell me exactly what you saw."

"Got off my shift at the GM plant in Newark around three o'clock and stopped here on my way home, like I usually do. I thought Rami was in back, but then I saw the feet and I thought he might have passed out or something." Chandler looked pale.

"What then?"

"Like I said, I thought Rami passed out or had a heart attack or something, so I ran over to see if I could help. Soon as I saw all that blood I got the hell out of there and called you guys." He breathed faster and his forehead grew slick.

"Did you check to see if he was still alive first?"

"Hey, I was in the service, and I know what a dead guy looks like, okay? Besides, I didn't want to stick around to see if there was anyone still in the store, you know what I mean? I have a wife and three kids."

"You called the victim by name. Did you know him well?"

"Just saw him once a day to buy coffee and the paper and shit like that. He wore a nametag. He had a strong accent, so we didn't have too many deep, meaningful conversations or nothing. His English wasn't good like yours."

"Thanks." Chang pushed aside memories of endless diction lessons and surprise tests at the dinner table by his father. "Did you see anything else out of place? Was anyone coming out of the parking lot when you pulled in?"

"No. That time of the morning the lot's usually empty."

Chang thanked him and verified contact information.

* * *

Back in the store, Burris peered down at Patel's body. He shook his head.

"Damndest thing I ever saw," Burris said.

"Why do you say that?" Chang's Uncle Tuen always told him that a wise man will jump at a chance to make amends.

"Robbery and some shootings I've seen, but that lemon thing is weird. The Staties got you from homicide in New York, right?"

"That's right." Chang stared at the mangled lemon perched on the victim's face.

"Thought so. Do you know what the crushed fruit means?"

"Not yet." Something buzzed in Chang's head. Why did this remind him of the Elsmere murders? Killer played with food there, too. Vietnamese use lemongrass in their cooking. Connection to the Nguyens?

"Well, that ought to break the case wide open. Good thing you stopped by. I think we got it from here." Burris showed his teeth.

"Excuse me?" Chang watched Burris puff out his chest. No more second chances.

Burris waved to the forensics team. "City limits, champ. This is ours. We'll call if we need any more New York perspective."

"I don't think so. You said it yourself. Unusual circumstances. I call it for State."

"The hell you say. How do you figure?"

Chang quelled the urge to flip Burris to the ground and instead affected an exaggerated Asian accent. "Confucius say: Man who turn face into juicer, not using food for thought."

"Huh?"

"I think this crime is tied to that double murder in Elsmere. I'm the lead on that investigation, and this case is now part of it." The small blue-collar town was outside city limits, but Burris wouldn't go quietly.

Burris planted his feet. "I don't agree." By now the forensics team, a short woman and tall man, watched and waited.

"And I don't need your consent. If you don't like it, take it up with the colonel. Until he says otherwise, this one is mine." Chang closed the distance and stared down Burris. When Burris looked away, Chang held out his hand for the clipboard to sign off on the body. The tall man gave it to him. Burris stood for a moment, and then Chang heard him grunt "Uppity slope..." under his breath and walk away.

An ambulance crew loaded Patel's body after the forensics team cleared it.

"Aside from the lemon on the victim, it looks like a straightforward shooting," the short technician said, jotting notes.

Her partner nodded agreement. "Two rounds to the subject's head, one slug likely still in the skull and one we have a chance at locating, given the size of the exit wound."

Chang wanted a second opinion. "Where was he when he got hit?"

"Facing the door." The short tech pointed to the fan of blood and tissue on the floor.

The killer made eye contact.

Chang aimed his finger at approximately head level for Patel. He scanned the wall. "There you are." Chang took out a pocket knife and gently dug around the hole. He pulled out a lead slug.

Chang held up the bullet to the lanky tech. "Looks like a .38, don't you think?"

"Good eye. It's a little deformed from the wall, but it looks too heavy to be a nine. We'll know more if the other one comes out of the victim."

Gilpin returned after thirty minutes. His uniform sported several large stains.

"Sir, if he ditched it nearby, it wasn't in any of the dumpsters I searched. Why did Burris say I shouldn't talk to you?"

"Never mind him. Thanks for the effort." Chang pressed a twenty into his hand. "For the cleaning bill."

When Chang drove off, he saw Gilpin wave. Burris stood nearby and shot Chang the finger.

CHAPTER 3
Overtime

A couple hours before dawn. No point going home; he wouldn't sleep. Chang pointed the unmarked car toward Quaker Hill. Never met a Quaker in this rough part of town, but he didn't seek pacifists when he walked the streets.

Chang parked on a lonely side street and tossed his shield in the glove box. His shift was over, and he felt the switch flip in his head. He got out of the car and felt the weight of his pistol under his armpit. In his mind, he let the facts flow from this and another puzzling murder. His instincts cried out that there had to be a connection. He wandered the empty sidewalks and relished the dark windows of the slumbering businesses. Like closed eyes. No judgment.

In half a month, two sets of murders that didn't fit the area norm. Two weeks ago the double murder at a Vietnamese grocery in Elsmere.

A Vietnamese immigrant couple, Tran and Min Nguyen, shot to death, execution style. Both tied up, seated in chairs, and each shot twice in the back of the head with a .22-caliber weapon. The empty cash register was no surprise; not so the merchandise in each victim's lap.

Chang figured the killer must have entered the small grocery store near closing time. Nobody reported anything until the Nguyens' son came by to work the early shift at the store the next morning.

Jason Nguyen had given clear answers through tears Chang knew he must have been embarrassed to shed in front of a stranger. His parents held a respected position in the community, and they owed no large debts. The store earned enough for a modest living. They'd just replaced their twelve-year-old Honda Civic with a new one they planned to drive for the next twelve. No life insurance, and Jason was their only son. Chang ruled him out as a suspect.

The photos of the cans and vegetables ran through his mind, block after block in the predawn gloom. He flashed back on the crushed lemon on Patel's face. What's the link? Must find one soon, or Burris and the locals would take the case away from him.

The weapon used to kill Patel was probably a .38, bigger than the .22 used on the Nguyens. Tied up and shot in the back of the head versus twice in the face. Takes more guts to look the victim in the eye, he knew.

The Patel shooting fit a robbery gone wrong, but the lemon rippled that surface appearance like a rock in a pond. Never saw a thief mash a fruit into a dead man's face. A message? A warning?

Jason Nguyen showed trust when he admitted to Chang that his parents paid "protection" money each month to a local Vietnamese organized crime group. He didn't think the kid noticed the way Chang's anger and sympathy swirled together in a poisonous blend.

Gangs... Chang noticed the stars fade at the first signs of dawn. The streets and alleys in this part of town reminded him of the gang-controlled territory of his youth. The signs were in English, but he could see his Uncle Tuen move inside the glass storefronts. Chang passed a pawnshop, and a small jade figurine on display reminded him of the way Tuen's long fingers would turn an antique piece over and over while he explained its history and spiritual meaning.

The image of his uncle's kind eyes and quick hands gave way to the hatchet-hacked nightmare left for Chang to discover. The Tongs had spoken: Pay up.

Did Jason Nguyen get the same message?

Uncle Tuen taught him to take all the indignities of life in Chinatown, white America, even the demands of his parents, and place them in a sphere in his heart. Chang could still hear his voice: "Concentrate on business. Do not give power to others; live well. Best revenge..."

Jason never saw anybody slip out the back door like Chang did so long ago. Maybe that was best. The sight of the killer and Tuen's body gave Chang his first glimpse of the Dragon. Tuen's sphere turned out to be what Chang thought of as an egg. The brutal murder caused it to hatch. The Dragon had a voice of its own, and the fury in Chang's chest said, *Payback.*

Police knew the local gang that shook down the Nguyens. For the most part it kept to zoning bribes, property scams, and questionable merchandise brought in through Philly. They didn't stand out for excessive violence against the tightly knit Vietnamese community in north Delaware.

Chang's face burned with shame in the cool morning air. After Uncle Tuen was killed, his father groveled to the

Tongs with bribes. Probably would have for the rest of his life if Chang hadn't repaid the Tongs and survived their own retaliation. Chang rubbed the thick cord of scar tissue that ran down his neck.

Were some of Jason's tears for the shame he felt?

He remembered the mixture of relief and embarrassment when Father sold the business and left New York for Delaware. Art professor was an honorable position, but why did he have to run from New York?

Chang and the Dragon wanted war; his father wanted peace. The price was too high either way, and Chang never managed to close the chasm before his father's heart gave out years later.

Pink light filtered through the early morning mist. Something about this case. Strange uses of food. Should he ask Nelson for help?

Nelson. His closest friend and biggest burden. Some days he wished the guy had stayed in New York, but Chang had brought him down here and thus felt responsible for him.

Now the man just holed up in his little town house in Bear and played with his dog. He told Chang he liked his job with the state. Chang knew he lied, but pretended not to notice. Nelson's cop days were over.

On the job, Nelson was like some sort of weird bloodhound for clues. At least before his breakdown. Was it fair to drag him out again?

* * *

The sound of breaking glass cut through the fog in Chang's mind. He strode toward the corner and heard muffled voices and a scream.

"Pull him out. Hit him again. Do it."

Chang neared the corner. The screamer moaned now. He heard a thump that reminded him of the way old ladies in Chinatown used to hang rugs out the windows and beat them with bamboo rods to clean them.

He poked his head around the wall. Two men with their backs to him, one with a bat. Long, straggly brown hair. Both white. On the ground, an elderly black man with a white, wooly head of hair. Dressed well, coat and tie. A bunch of keys lay on the ground in front of a pharmacy door.

The old man met Chang's gaze for an instant. Pain and terror. Chang felt the Dragon stir in his chest.

CHAPTER 4

In the Grip of the Dragon

One final kick and the old man lay on his chest, unconscious. The jackals still didn't know Chang was there.

"Get the key. Hurry up."

Chang smelled the spicy jasmine oil from Tuen's shop. He felt the scales of the Dragon slide through the bars of its cage and fill his chest, arms, legs, head…

One of the animals fiddled with the keys. Shaky fingers, all twitchy and hungry. The other, thick and strong, held the bat. Heard the footfalls and turned. "Dude."

The skinny one jumped and gave a little feral snarl. He reached into his back pocket and flicked open a knife. The big one smiled and rested the bat on his shoulder.

"Well, well, well. You here to get your vities nice and early?" Both hands on his bat.

Pinpoint eyes. Probably high. Won't feel as much pain… Yes, he will.

"Speaky English?" Poked the bat at his stomach.

Rapid laugh from the knife guy.

"Don't run." Chang heard the flat voice that came out of his own mouth. He felt like an observer.

"Don't worry." Baseball bat came at him, looked like it was in slow motion, and Chang watched his own foot lash out to catch the big guy in the knee. He barely registered the off-balance blow on his shoulder and felt something give in the guy's leg. Howl of pain and the guy fell. The aluminum bat clattered on the sidewalk.

Knife. Chang leapt back from the silvery flash that arced along his side. He didn't feel a cut but was beyond pain. Maybe later.

"Evan, get up! Fucker's quick," Skinny said.

Evan rolled on the ground and clutched his knee. Skinny gripped the knife and stabbed at Chang's midsection. Chang backed up a couple steps, and Skinny kept jabbing with the knife. The old man groaned again. Not dead. Good. Chang let Skinny get closer, and when he tried to stab him again, he turned sideways, parried the knife arm, and grabbed it by the wrist.

He used Skinny's momentum and redirected him face-first into the stone wall of a building. He held the wrist with his left hand and twisted Skinny's fingers with his right until Skinny shrieked and dropped the knife.

Chang kicked the knife away and began to crush the fingers. The Dragon sent wave after wave of adrenaline into his hands. The sound of snapped pencils filled the air. Skinny dropped to his knees. Blood ran down his face, and he cradled his mangled hand. A hard knee to the side of his head was all it took to ease his pain. Chang yanked the reins of the Dragon before it tried to finish Skinny off. He was able to turn its gaze toward Evan.

Evan was crawling down the block. Chang waited for him to try to get up. When Evan started to hop, he closed the distance. Evan raised his hands.

"Dude, you win. I didn't get anything off the guy. Let me go."

Another sound from the old man.

"Dude, you broke my fucking leg. All right?"

No. Be quick.

Evan tried to run and fell. When he began to crawl, Chang saw his own shoe flash into the beefy ribcage, once, twice, three times. Enough. He yanked on the reins with every ounce of his will. Evan was either too hurt to move or smart enough not to entice the Dragon again. Chang ran back and checked on the old man. He wasn't awake, but his vital signs were strong. Chang found a pay phone and used his shirt to muffle his voice when he called for an ambulance. He wiped the receiver with his sleeve.

The Dragon slid back into its cage to digest its meal. Chang stepped into an alley and vomited his dinner onto the oily bricks.

CHAPTER 5

When a Stranger Calls

The Wilmington Daily Post

Usually Patrick Flannigan sucked on his cigarette until he could taste the filter. He hated the new rule that banished smokers out onto the gulag of a concrete square behind the newspaper's main building. When he dragged his bones outside, rain or shine, he made it count. Not today.

He ground out the cigarette with his heel and left the butt next to the sand bucket. Screw 'em. He wasn't the fucking janitor. He also wasn't the joke the sales team thought he was. Their meeting was about to end, and the most obnoxious of them would rush out here to share a smoke with the "Hunchback of Notre Dame." Little shits. His alma mater would have rejected half of them. Let them live with osteoporosis for a month and get back to him with bell-ringer jokes.

His column, "The Blarney Stone," may not have had the following it once did, but it still sold papers. He held no illusions about what would happen if he lost the rest of his readers. Since last week he didn't think that was going to be a problem.

"I've got a seeeecret..." He could still hear the voice from over a week ago. He remembered the charge he felt at the muffled words. He got his share of crank calls, but right away he smelled a headline. His instincts weren't dead yet.

"Want to know more about the two yellow worms killed last night?"

"You know something that wasn't in the paper?"

"Everything..." Excitement in the voice.

Flannigan mouthed a silent prayer. He only needed a little luck. "Why me and not the beat reporter?"

"I like your stuff."

A fan.

The voice gave him specifics about the killings far beyond what appeared in the paper. Flannigan had contacts in the department. It would only take a moment to check them out. It would only take a moment to check them out. It would also be a simple matter to get the information the caller wanted as part of his offer.

"Here's the deal. If you work with me, I'll give you the first look at my gifts. I think I'm supposed to make the world a better place, and I need to share with someone I can trust."

"What do you want from me?" The phone felt slick in his hand.

"First a test. I see the article listed some cop named Chang on the case. I want his full name, home address, and phone number."

"I can't..." Flannigan's protest was reflexive.

"Don't insult me. You aren't supposed to, but you can. What do you say? Or should I call the *Inquirer*?"

"No." Flannigan hated the pleading tone that jumped in front of his usual smoky bark of a voice. "I'll need a day."

Just like that, he knew he'd taken his first step of a long journey. He didn't care where it led if he made it back to the big time.

"Good. I'll call you back tomorrow. You give me the information, fast as you can. If you try to keep me on the line, I'll hang up and make you my top priority, understand?"

"Get in line behind the Marlboro man." Flannigan tried to laugh but instead lapsed into a spasm of coughs.

"Tomorrow, then? If what you tell me checks out, we can do business."

"Wait. Use my cell." Flannigan gave him the number. Even the paper didn't know about this phone.

Sure enough, the guy called back. Same muffled voice. Flannigan checked with his source. The caller knew too many details to be a prankster. The guy was for real. Flannigan kept his voice steady when he gave him the information, and he even tossed in the cop's mother's address. The line went dead the instant he finished with Chang's phone number.

He knew he couldn't warn the cop, not directly. He thought about how he might try. An anonymous call? Nah. He'd seen a picture of Chang once. Big bastard, especially for a Chinese guy. He was supposed to be hot shit anyway. He could take care of himself.

Flannigan returned to his desk and rubbed the cell phone in his pocket. He had a feeling it wouldn't be long before it would ring. Call it a reporter's instinct.

CHAPTER 6
Chip Shot

Chang walked into the information department where Nelson worked. Clusters of cubicles chopped up the open workspace, and he made his way through the rat maze. Blonde hair caught his eye, and he was too late to turn away before a familiar face looked up.

"Hey, cutie! I didn't know you were coming down here. How did you find me?" The woman stood, and her ponytail bobbed.

Chang let her hug him while he searched his recent memory. Dover Downs Lounge, aggressive, a back-scratcher. Had her number at home. Janet? Janice? Forgot she worked for the state… "Hi. Just good luck. I'm here to meet a friend, a guy."

"It better be a guy." She gave him a little punch on the arm. "You should call me. We can go dancing or something."

Or something. He skimmed his eyes over her desk and saw her nameplate. Janelle. If he could find the number maybe he would. "Sure. I've been busy…"

"It's cool. No need to explain. You have my number."

He caught her defensive tone. Time to go.

"Absolutely. You take care." He kissed her cheek and ignored the stares of the other women nearby. He made a mental note not to pass this direction on the way out.

* * *

When Chang reached the other side of the huge room, he could see his friend's back while he tapped on a keyboard. Gray streaked the unmistakable home-cut black hair, and ragged tufts circled his oversized head.

Nelson chomped on a cookie. A second "care package" of brownies sat untouched on top of the computer monitor. The ladies in his office were always leaving home-baked goods on Nelson's desk, but Nelson looked thinner than ever. Chang pushed away a twinge of guilt. Too often he stayed away from this side of the building just to avoid his old partner.

Betty, the nosy soccer mom in the next cubicle, peered over the wall. "Nelson, what did you get for four letters across, Moro letter opener?"

"Kris." Nelson took another bite, and Chang saw the completed puzzle, in pen, on his desk.

"Chris?" She counted the letters on her hand.

Nelson continued to type while he spoke. "With a K. Knife with a wavy blade."

"Oh. Thanks." She ducked back behind the wall.

Chang kept his voice low. "You ready for tonight?"

This startled Nelson, who swiveled around in his chair. His dark eyes met Chang's. He wiped cookie crumbs off his mouth. "Does it matter?" Nelson stared harder at Chang, who gestured for him to follow. "Hey..."

No point sharing with the whole office. Chang led Nelson away from eager ears.

"What happened to you?" There was concern in Nelson's voice, but at least he whispered.

"It's nothing."

"You're hurt. Your side, isn't it?"

Nelson's uncanny powers of observation could chafe worse than the leather strap of his shoulder holster. The punk's cut wasn't deep, but it went right under the rig for his compact Kimber .45. An inch higher and his gun would have hit the sidewalk that night. Another inch deeper and he might not be here. Fate had its own schedule.

"I said I'm fine."

Nelson's eyes were the only locus of strength on his scrawny frame. "The Dragon? Don't answer; I don't want to know."

Chang knew Nelson had never seen the Dragon up close.

"Did you read the poker booklet I gave you?" Chang was going to drag Nelson to this game if he had to cuff him.

"I still don't know what I'm doing. Why do you need me there, anyway?"

"You never get out of the house, and I need someone I can beat. It'll be good for you." Chang didn't know how to explain his Asian sense of responsibility for him. Shu understood.

Chang wanted a friendly face for his first time as host. He'd played once before with the troopers from the elite Special Operations and Response Team (SORT) unit, Delaware's answer to a SWAT team. They first surprised Chang with an invite to play, then again when they accepted his offer to host. He knew Nelson would be uncomfortable around other cops who looked more like marines, but Chang had to do something to bring him back to the world.

"You'll do fine. You don't even need to know the game. Just watch their eyes." The human lie detector.

"I can't always read you."

More than he'd like, but Shu's teachings paid off.

"They're not so different. You catch killers, something in common with that crew." Chang saw Nelson's shoulders sag.

"I *used* to. Now I catch computer bugs." Nelson sounded resigned. "Seven tonight?"

"Don't be late."

CHAPTER 7

In the Fold

Wilmington

Chang liked that the fieldstone exterior and professional landscaping enabled his house to blend into the quiet neighborhood. Its four bedrooms surpassed his needs, but the home had once housed two with the hope of more.

Inside, he was proud of the changes, and he thought even Colleen would approve of the way he finished what she started with the feng shui. In the front hallway he installed black shelves that set off the pale antique jade figures of dragons and Buddha. He drew from their smooth strength. Chang looked at the wall scrolls that showcased famous warriors from several dynasties. The formal dining room featured paintings with bamboo and other trees to incorporate green elements. Teak and cherry furniture met the wood requirement on his feng shui *bagua* map.

He was especially pleased with his collection of Chinese masks that lined the upstairs hallway and his bedroom. Colleen always complained that the brightly colored masks stared at her during lovemaking. He took them down for her, but after she left for good they were back up by the end of the day.

The Asian artwork throughout his home was a more aesthetic reminder of his heritage than the late-night visits to his mother's.

Chang heard his doorbell and knew it was Nelson because he pushed the button like it gave him a shock. Most of the crew was already waiting downstairs.

In the kitchen, after letting Nelson in, Chang grabbed a tray of chips and pretzels. Not many guests since Colleen left.

"Take that cooler," he said. Nelson grunted from the effort.

In the basement, two guys who could have been Marine Corps bookends sat at a circular card table. Tate and Wiggins. A hanging lamp cast a pool of light on the green felt in the long room. A heavy punching bag hung in the far corner. The men looked up and stared.

They were both Chang's height, about six-four, their bodies as chiseled as his. Both wore SORT sweatshirts. Nelson looked like a clothes hanger compared to them. Chang left Nelson to let in the last player, Carl Hull.

Where the twenty-something Wiggins and Tate were bodybuilders, Carl was a power lifter with massive shoulders and a large stomach. Hull was their boss on the SORT team.

"Evening, Cap," the pair said in unison. Hull nodded and crossed the room.

"Beer, Paul?" Hull held out a can to Chang and opened one for himself.

"Maybe one, thanks. I get all red in the face if I have more." Never mind what they thought. Booze lubricated the bars on the Dragon's cage.

"I could use a cold one." Nelson grabbed the can and took a big pull. Chang saw his eyes water. Nelson was no drinker.

Chang sipped his beer.

"Let's get started." Chang pulled out a deck of cards and began to shuffle them. A tray of poker chips sat on the table. "Nothing fancy, a quarter ante, and let's say a dollar limit per hand, okay?"

"We'll go slow for you, Nelson," Tate said.

Chang didn't know a good way to warn them. "Nelson may surprise you."

"Might not." Nelson hit the beer again.

Nelson lagged early, but soon he barely looked at his cards and instead watched faces. He began to win and folded whenever another player held a strong hand. Chang knew Nelson could read subtle cues from the other players.

There was nothing subtle about the frustration on the men's faces. Their polite amusement at the strange little man wore off when he continued to win. Nelson stopped asking for cards. He sipped his beer and stared at the other players.

Wiggins drank heavily all night, and Chang didn't need Nelson's sensitivity to see his anger. On one hand, everyone but Wiggins and Nelson folded. The biggest pot of the night sat between them.

"Showdown. Come on, Wiggins, win one for the team here," Hull said.

"After you," Nelson said.

"You're bluffing. You got nothing, and I'm taking the pot with this junk." Wiggins turned his cards over and showed a pair of threes. When Nelson showed fives, Wiggins's face flushed red.

Chang's pulse picked up.

"Bullshit. That's a trick. What are you, a magician?" Wiggins pulled down the last three-quarters of his beer and crushed the can.

Nelson stifled a belch. "Not my fault. You told me what you had."

"You were really a cop?" Wiggins looked at Nelson like it was the first time he'd noticed him. "Special operations or Special Olympics?" He snorted and looked around at his friends.

"New York's finest."

"For how long?"

"Too long."

Chang sat still. Pressure began to build in his chest.

"Yeah? What kind of weapon did you carry?"

"Air pistol." On the job, Nelson invariably failed surprise inspections because he left his gun at home and wore an empty holster.

Wiggins frowned. "You ever kick in a door and make an arrest?"

"Nope."

"Ever land a guy after a vehicle pursuit?"

"In New York, bad guys take the subways. You must not get out of Delaware much."

"You ever catch *any*body?"

"Sometimes."

"How'd you arrest 'em? Probably had guys like me watch your back and do the dirty work so you wouldn't get hurt."

Nelson faced Wiggins. "Sort of. They didn't call me 'Nervous Nelly' for nothing."

Chang heard a touch of a Brooklyn accent creep into Nelson's voice. "Nervous" came out "Noy-vus." It only happened when he was excited or angry. Between foster homes, Nelson was educated in a Catholic orphanage. Chang knew that a diminutive nun "beat the accent out of him," as Nelson liked to put it.

Chang's own father spent a fortune to make sure his son received a firm grounding in the King's English. Father's obsession that Chang sound neither Asian nor like a New Yorker worked. What Father called "better" everyone else called different.

Nelson's body language made Chang think of a bowstring. Chang saw him lean toward Wiggins and say, "Good news or bad news? Don't be scared, Wiggins."

"Of what? You?" Wiggins sounded tough, but his eyes showed uncertainty.

Nelson gestured toward Tate and Hull. "Good news is that one of your friends doesn't think you're weak." Nelson looked at the two. "I won't say which one. It'll be our secret..."

Wiggins started to stand.

Chang heard his own chair fall when he sprang up. "Sit down or come after me." Hull and Tate put their hands on Wiggins's shoulders, and he sank back into his seat. His expression told Chang that the Nelson-style sucker punch hit a nerve.

Nelson turned to Chang.

"Thanks for inviting me." He nodded to rest of the group. "Gentlemen, enjoy the rest of your game."

The bowstring went slack.

"Hold on." Chang followed Nelson up the stairs and into the front hallway.

"I don't belong with those guys."

"I don't know what Wiggins's problem is, but I'm going to find out." Chang felt the thunderheads build.

"Doesn't matter."

"He thinks that any cop who isn't part jarhead doesn't rate. I'll make sure he gets it." Whatever it takes.

"I don't want his pity."

"For what? I'll straighten these guys out."

"Just leave it." Nelson dropped his gaze.

Chang couldn't allow Nelson to withdraw.

"No. Good cops come in all shapes and sizes." Even skeletal geniuses. "I might need your help."

"What's that supposed to mean?"

"Later. Go home." Chang closed the door before Nelson could say anything else.

Chang's anger sought release. Couldn't go downstairs yet… Chang strode into the kitchen. Above the sink on a small shelf sat "Banzai," the bonsai tree Colleen had given him in what turned out to be one of her last real efforts to salvage their relationship. Named after her mispronunciation, he insisted on keeping it even after she tried to discard it when she realized it was part of Japanese culture, not Chinese.

Chang took the tiny scissors off the wall and began to prune the tree. His hand felt more like a talon, Dragon-strength making the shears seem clumsy.

Sometimes it relaxed him, and he was determined not to embarrass himself in front of his colleagues. While he worked he pictured a stream and clear, cool water flowing over his anger...

Chang's reverie broke when he saw that he'd just hacked half the branches down to the trunk. He flung the scissors into the sink and tossed the maimed tree into the trash can. He glanced at the clock and saw it had only taken him five minutes to ruin a seventy-five-year-old dwarf pine.

* * *

When he went downstairs, Chang could hear Wiggins's voice above the others.

"...find that guy, anyway? What does he see in him? He couldn't arrest a jaywalker." Wiggins broke off when he saw Chang.

"Let's get one thing clear. When you are in my house, you will respect the other guests." He kept his voice even.

"Hey, I didn't mean to run the guy off. I was just messing with him. Is he sick or something? You shoulda told me he was so thin-skinned."

"I'll tell you why right now."

Everyone pulled up a chair.

* * *

After the last guest left, Chang finished his cleanup. It helped to restore order to his home. Then he put on a scarlet silk robe. He never liked dredging up New York, but he wanted the men to understand what he and Nelson had endured.

He'd told them he wondered if Nelson didn't have some sort of undiagnosed high-functioning autism. His ability to think like a killer dueled with his inability to relate to regular people.

Before his breakdown, Nelson could act "normal" when he wanted to—the only reason he made it through the academy. The brass must have laughed when they forced "Nervous Nelly" and "Bang-Bang Chang" to partner.

Their success and ultimate failure was a matter of record. Even after the smear job following the Topper murder, anyone could read the newspapers and understand they were an effective team.

Operative word: *were.* If he dragged Nelson back into the game, who was it for?

Chang stared at the remains of Banzai. He couldn't throw it away with the empty beer cans. The side he hadn't cut looked healthy. Maybe he could nurse it back…

Chang heard a metallic sound from outside. It took a moment to register: the lid to his garbage can. Raccoon?

He tiptoed into his dining room to look out from a darkened window. He didn't want to spook the animal yet. He saw a large, dark shape bent over one can, and when it stood up he saw a dark mask and white eyes. Not an animal. Someone was going through his trash.

Tongs? Stupid. They come with knives while you sleep. They're not here in Delaware. Who is this?

Chang raced to the kitchen and pulled the lid off a joke gift jar that showed a fat Buddha and said "Fortune Cookies." Another Colleen relic. Chang reached inside and pulled out his backup weapon, a .38 revolver.

He yanked open his back door and jumped down the few steps to the ground. He ignored the pebble that dug into his bare foot.

The man was all in black, and his surprise registered in the huge white eyes that leapt out from the dark mask. In one hand he held not a weapon but a fistful of paper.

"Hey!" Chang lunged at the dark figure. Winos don't wear masks. He didn't move like a Tong, either.

The man jumped at Chang's yell and ran when he approached. He flipped the can over into Chang's path. The silk robe tugged at his legs, and Chang tripped.

He skinned his hand and scrambled to his feet, but by then the guy had a full head of steam. Chang raised the pistol, and the light at the end of the alley gave him a perfect sight picture. You can't shoot…

He exploded into a full sprint before the thought was completed and saw the dark outline dart around the corner. By the time Chang reached the street he could hear dogs barking, but he saw no sign of the snoop. Chang's lungs burned and his hand stung, but he knew better than to stumble around in the dark anymore tonight. He picked a piece of broken glass out of his foot and pulled one arm into a sleeve to conceal the gun. He froze in the shadows when a back porch light snapped on. His injured foot throbbed.

When the light turned off, he was able to reach his back door. Who *was* that? Identity thief? He stayed in his kitchen until his foot stopped bleeding. Before bed, he remembered to wipe off the blood he'd smeared on the back steps.

CHAPTER 8

Due Diligence

Greenville, just north of Wilmington

Shamus Ryan squirmed sitting on the ice in the rectangular baking pan. The towel protected the battered chair, but his boxer shorts were soaking wet. Tough. Gran may have dropped dead in the icehouse, but he brought her along in spirit. His carelessness had earned this punishment.

He looked over the sheaf of papers he'd swiped from the trash can. The big cop scared him. He looked like some sort of Asian superhero in that red silk robe. Shamus should have brought his gun, but he was glad he'd planned an escape route.

He loved cyber cafés. A couple hours of research and he knew Chang's story.

The number of articles surprised him and also that many of them came from New York. The headlines screamed off the paper: "Dynamic Duo Split Apart," "Topper Drops Cops," "Fratricide Shooting Ruled Accident: Chang Cleared, Questions Remain," "Lateral Move No Demotion, Chief Claims."

Chang was a hero in New York before he and his partner, some guy named Rogers, blew a kidnapping case. The girl, some spoiled bitch named Jennifer Topper, got snatched and her rich daddy had the whole NYPD chasing its tail. Shamus loved that a big-shot real estate mogul was forced to grovel and depend on the cops, who of course let him down. They found her body dumped on a tennis court. Nice touch. The killer had style. Too bad Chang shot him, but he screwed that up too. He killed another cop in all the confusion. Too funny!

The guy on his case was the same Chang who couldn't figure anything out till this girl was meat on a slab. That's the "Decorated Officer Comes to Delaware" he should be worried about? Shamus smiled and lifted his butt off the ice.

Chang's partner was so broken up he'd left the force altogether. One reporter even hinted that this Nelson Rogers had a nervous breakdown. Apparently, he was the brains and this big Chinese guy was the muscle. If so, Shamus had no worries. Let the imbeciles put their stock in an overgrown retread. Now he knew his competition.

Enough discipline. Tomorrow was the best sales day of the week.

* * *

Saturday, another glorious spring day, and Shamus was anxious to get to the dealership. One chore left.

He hung a huge corkboard on the bedroom wall with newspaper clippings pinned to it. So far, the few articles contained either the name Patel or Nguyen. Room for many more. All artists start with a blank canvas, don't they? He knew Gran would find a way to send him others.

He reserved a special section for "The Blarney Stone." She would have loved Flannigan's style.

Shamus wanted a fast start this morning. With a quick sale in the morning, the rest of the day would just fall into place. The customers could smell the success on him.

He jumped into his trusty Honda, proof positive of the reliability of the products he sold. The ten-year-old car had racked up more than 170,000 miles on it. He wanted to replace it, but he needed more consistent income. He lived just down the road from Patriot Motors and arrived in plenty of time for the sales meeting.

"Shamus, you made it! All right! How ya doin', man?" Jonah boomed when Shamus came in the door.

Jonah, a short, thin black man, had hit sixty but packed the energy of a twenty-year-old. Shamus fed off his enthusiasm.

"I'm better than good. You ready to go today?" Shamus tried to match Jonah's wattage.

The rest of the crew filtered in. Sales champ Tom Panzer looked neat, but his red eyes gave away a late night. All the better, Shamus thought. At least *his* new drug didn't give him a hangover. Avery Fitz walked in at his usual steady pace, covering ground more gracefully than his bulk should have allowed. He weighed more than four hundred pounds and was on parole for a real estate sales scam that had gotten him a stretch in prison.

Hank Grant, the assistant manager, lived for silk ties and upscale food. He promised to talk to Avery later about the restaurant he tried last night. Shamus could hardly wait.

Jake, the ex–college linebacker and current sales manager, called everyone into the break room for the usual Saturday combination chew-out and pep talk. He praised

Tommy "the Tank" for his lead on the sales board and called attention to Shamus's recent efforts.

"Famous Shamus here is pulling in close; he's really turning it on. What's your secret?"

"Can't let the bastards get you down, sir."

"Attaboy, that's the spirit!" Jonah slapped Shamus on the back and jerked his thumb toward a glum, hard-working salesman named Mark Dey.

"Hey, you should take a lesson from Shamus here. I see you. You get too upset. You need to be like the Irish duck and let everything roll off your back." Jonah's laugh rang through the small room.

Someone started to sing the theme from *Howdy Doody,* and Shamus forced a smile. He hated the comparison that followed wherever he went. At least now he had an outlet.

When he was a kid, he didn't know which was worse—the dirt Gran made him eat for backing down from bullies or the cigarette burns she put on his legs for fighting back and causing school officials to bring her in.

Shamus popped a mint to drive the taste of earth out of his mouth.

The meeting ended, and the salesmen filed into the showroom to let in the early birds. The shiny new cars in the glassed-in box reminded Shamus of decorations on the bottom of an aquarium.

The doors opened, and the salesmen observed the protocol of taking customers in the order of who showed up to work first. Mark took the first up, a middle-aged man with his daughter. The second was a Chinese couple. Jonah took them, and Shamus was on deck.

Five minutes later, a rusted Chevy Caprice turned the corner and pulled into the parking lot. Older car, both decision-makers inside—buyers, had to be!

Shamus sat at the up desk by the front door. In walked an enormously overweight couple. The man wasn't a rival to Avery but easily north of three hundred pounds, and his wife wasn't far south.

"Hi, welcome to Patriot Motors. Is this your first time here?" Shamus put on his most radiant smile. His hand thrust out.

"Yeah."

"Great. I'm Shamus, and you are?"

"Doug Hubbert, and this is my wife, Maisy." She shook Shamus's hand.

Shamus resisted the urge to wipe his palm after shaking the sweaty paw she offered.

"What are you looking for today?"

"We need a new car, but we don't know much about the Hondas. What can you tell us?" Doug asked.

"Are you looking for a sedan, a minivan, or something else?"

"A car, but we don't want to spend a lot," Maisy said.

"Let me direct you over to our Civic line, which offers outstanding value." Shamus led the pair over to a four-door Civic on the showroom floor.

"It looks small," Maisy said.

"It's surprisingly roomy on the inside." Shamus glanced over and saw Tommy greet a young couple pushing a baby in a stroller. They went right to the minivan brochures. "Here, hop in and see how it feels." Shamus moved the seat all the way back to try to make room for her bulk. Maisy squeezed in, and the steering wheel pressed against her stomach.

"No, I still have more room in my Caprice. The seat feels tight." Her whiny tone grated on Shamus. Doug crammed his frame into the passenger seat, and Shamus heard the car settle on its suspension.

"Maybe we need the next bigger model," Doug said. "Is that the Accord?"

"Yes, sir. The Accord will give you more space, more power in the engine, and more comfort features. It has a number of levels, ranging from a base model up to a V6 with leather and luxury." Maybe he could move these customers up to the more expensive models. Now Hank welcomed an older couple who went straight to the Accords. They sounded like they were ready to buy today. Why was everyone else getting the dream walk ups?

"I'm not sure this car would be right for me because of my condition," Maisy said.

Shamus wasn't sure exactly what she meant by "condition" other than fat as freaking hell, but he figured he should agree with her.

"Let's take a look at this Accord." Shamus used his most diplomatic tone. The pair extracted themselves from the Civic and Shamus thought the suspension sounded grateful.

He showed them a mid-level Accord.

"How's that? Better?"

She shrugged.

"Tell you what. Let's get one out on the road." He took their flaccid nods as agreement.

"I'll be right back with an LX with the four-cylinder engine. If you think you'll want more power, we can go to the V6." Shamus led them to his desk.

Out on the lot, he saw Mark return from a test drive with the young woman, who was all smiles, and her father. Mark winked at him from the back seat. Shamus spotted the gold Accord in the front row and pulled the sedan in front of the dealership.

After a couple minutes Doug came through the door followed by Maisy. Though the temperature was mild, both were sweaty by the time they got to the car. Shamus stepped out of the sedan and held the door open for Maisy.

Shamus gave his best smile. Doug plopped into the front passenger seat. "Note how you can adjust the steering wheel to tilt it up or down." Away from your flabby stomach. "How is that? All set?"

"I guess so," Mrs. Blob said.

Shamus climbed into the back seat and pointed out the test drive route to Maisy. They turned left and headed away from downtown.

"I try to take folks out of the city and give them a chance to experience the car on a variety of roads so you can get a feel for how it handles. How does it feel so far, Maisy?"

"It feels good, peppy engine, the seat's pretty comfortable." Finally!

"Does this have navigation?" Doug asked.

"This model doesn't, but if a navigation system is important to you, it is available on our minivan, the Odyssey." Shamus hoped he could turn him onto a more profitable minivan. It would make his whole day!

"It isn't. I was just wondering. Does Honda pick up the first three years of maintenance? I think Mercedes does." He twisted in his seat to look at Shamus.

Mercedes? What the hell was this guy talking about? He drove a rotten Caprice and now he wanted a Benz?

"Uh, no, sir, it doesn't, but the Honda only requires oil changes every 7,500 miles, and the car is a perennial favorite of magazines like *Consumer Reports* in many areas, especially in terms of maintenance." That ought to shut him up. "Also keep in mind that you have to pay considerably more for a Mercedes, and part of that premium goes towards the so-called 'free' maintenance."

"I like that it's free."

So much for logic.

"I want to try one of these with the leather and the V6," Doug said.

"Okay, we can sure do that. While we have this one out, would you like to take a turn at the wheel so you can feel the four-cylinder?" This guy felt like a car shuffler.

"No, I want to try the six-cylinder. I can drive this later if I want."

But of course.

"I think you'll like the V6." Why couldn't he just try this car now? These people better buy!

Maisy took the car back and didn't say a word.

"Hang on for a minute while I get the keys to that silver V6 right over there."

"Does it come in bright red?" Doug said.

"I like red," Maisy said.

Shamus stopped. "Actually, the bright red is only available on the two-door Accords. The sedans have more of a maroon color. Is that okay?"

"No maroon," Maisy said.

Shamus winced inside. "Is silver out of the question?"

"No, I like silver, too," Doug said. Shamus felt revived.

"Great, I'll be right back with keys." He ducked into the showroom.

He noticed that Mark had closed his customer and Hank had scheduled a delivery. Tommy the Tank was showing a CR-V, Honda's compact SUV, to another young couple. They ate up his presentation. Shamus grabbed the keys from the cabinet in Jake's office and saw that Tommy had already sold an Odyssey to the people from earlier. Damn. He'd have to move it to catch up, and these whales were taking forever!

He returned to the Hubberts in the main lot.

"I'm back. Let me get the car off the lot, and we'll give Doug a chance to drive." Come on! He refused to get blanked today.

"Does the leather come in other colors?" Maisy asked.

Shamus gritted his teeth.

"Actually, the interior designs are preset by Honda. What color leather did you have in mind?" He smiled because it seemed like he should.

"I don't know. I just wanted to see some other colors is all. I mean, if we're going to pay all that money for a new car, we should get what we want."

"Of course you should. Why don't we get the car out on the road, and Doug, you can decide if you like the feel of the V6."

Doug took the car along the same route as before and seemed to pay no attention to Shamus's explanations of the features. He put the silver car through its paces. Shamus was sure he liked it. He'd know once they got back to the dealership.

CHAPTER 9
Bulk Order

"Does it feel like you could enjoy this car for the next few years?" Shamus used a classic "trial closing" question.

"I'm not sure," Doug said. "I want to try the four-cylinder car now."

Shamus bit the inside of his cheek. He expected the blood to burn his tongue.

Inside, out of sight of the Hubberts, he saw on the board that Mark and Tommy had added another sale each on the tally. Even the new kid notched a sale. It was now almost twelve thirty, and they closed at five.

"Hey, Famous Shamus, what's going on with those people?" Jake managed to yell without raising his voice.

"Jake, they won't pick a car. I know they like the V6, but the guy keeps taking cars out."

"Land them on a car and close them. They want you to take control. Be the man!"

Shamus ran back out and grabbed the gold Accord again.

"Okay, Doug, let's go."

Maisy lumbered into the passenger side, and soon they were off on the test route.

“This feels underpowered,” Doug said.

“We need more power.” Maisy sounded like a whiny parrot.

“That settles it, then.” Shamus took control. “The V6 it is. Let’s go back and put together a terrific deal for you. Are you planning to trade in your old car?”

“No, we’re selling it to her sister,” Doug said. “She’s kind of big, and she needs a car that she can fit in.”

Shamus suppressed a shudder at the mental picture.

“I’m hungry.” Maisy sounded like a petulant child.

“Okay, honey, you want to get some lunch and come back?”

No! They’ll never come back if they leave now. Shamus had to think of something.

“We don’t have much longer to go, but if it will help, I have a sandwich. Why don’t you have that and some pretzels while I get my manager to work up a great price for you? I’ll make it worth your time.” Shamus ignored his empty stomach’s protest.

“I don’t know…” Doug looked over at Maisy.

“What kind of sandwich?” Maisy fixed beady eyes on Shamus.

“Turkey with swiss, I think, on wheat bread.”

“All right, as long as it doesn’t take too long.”

“Yeah, tell your guy we don’t have all day,” Doug said.

Could have fooled him.

“Great! Come back inside and get your snack.”

He seated them at his desk and ducked back into the break room to retrieve his lunch. He handed the paper bag over to Maisy and began to fill out a buyer’s order. He stopped when he realized that Maisy was staring at him.

“Is something wrong?”

"You don't expect me to eat without something to drink, do you?"

"Of course, where are my manners?" Shamus smiled and hoped they couldn't see the vein in his forehead begin to throb. "Is a Pepsi okay?"

"Diet, if you have it."

"No problem." Like that will make a difference. He returned shortly with two cans of soda.

"I'll be right back. Enjoy." He heard the lunch bag tear.

When Shamus got into Jake's office, he found Jake staring through the window that gave him a view of all the cubicles. His look was one of disbelief. Shamus followed his gaze.

The Hubberts were devouring his lunch. Doug made half the sandwich go away in three quick bites, and Maisy used both hands to shovel pretzels into her mouth. For a moment Shamus forgot why he was there.

"Here's their buyer's order for that silver V6. We have to hurry before she eats my desk."

"At least you landed them on a car. Good job." Jake shook his head in disbelief. He wrote a number to open negotiations. "Here you go; now don't lose them. You've spent all day with them, so that shows they like you. Go get 'em."

"Hey, just because you feed a stray doesn't mean it likes you." Shamus geared up for combat, and Jake chuckled.

"Thanks for your patience, folks." He tried to appear relaxed and cleared a spot on his desk amidst the carnage. Pretzel crumbs were strewn everywhere, even on Maisy's mouth. Shamus did his best to ignore them.

"Now, here's what the car normally sells for." He pointed to the paper. "Since you spent so much time with us, Jake wanted to make sure you got a good deal."

After a long pause Doug said, "That's way more than we want to spend. We were thinking more like the price on the LX we drove."

"I understand. Would you like me to write up the gold car we drove to save you some money?"

"No. I want the V6 and the leather, but if you want our business, you're going to have to come close to the price on the gold one."

"That's a different model, Doug. But if you work with me here, we can meet somewhere in the middle and try to convince my manager to go for it." Shamus could see his commission race toward a "mini-deal," a lousy hundred bucks. Damn!

"Do whatever you have to. Tell your manager if he wants to sell a car today, he'll do what's right." Doug spoke with righteous conviction.

"If I could get him to split the difference, would you take the car? That is a great deal." The vein on his forehead was back.

"Go ask him and tell me what he says," Doug said. Shamus could feel himself lose control.

He needed a break, even though Doug refused to offer a good-faith deposit.

"Shamus!" Jake yelled, for real this time. "He's playing you! He can afford the car; he's just sweating you, and you gave in and came back here to Daddy!" He looked at the clock. "Christ, it's after two, and everyone else is selling cars. Close this guy. He ate your lunch, and you're just going to take that?" He crossed out the figure and dropped from his original offer.

Shamus returned and smiled. "Wow, he did better than I thought. He came down a bunch. I thought we were aiming a little low, but this way now we know." Shamus was sure they'd get down to it now. Victory at last.

"That's no good," Maisy said.

"What do you mean? That's a tremendous price." He looked at Doug. "You need to work with me here. I can't do all the dropping; that isn't right."

"Seems fair from here," Doug said, and Maisy screeched laughter. Several salesmen looked over.

"Like I said, if you want to sell me this car, you're going to have to earn it." He produced a hundred-dollar bill with a flourish. "You tell your manager that since you took all my time today I want to make it worth my while, so here's my deposit and I'll buy the car for this price." Doug pointed.

Shamus presented the cash to Jake. "These people are unbelievable. I don't know what he's thinking, but he's locked in. We still may have a shot if we move a little." Mark was in the office waiting to present another buyer's order.

"I could hear them, Jake. They're nuts," Mark said. Shamus was grateful for the support.

Jake scowled and consulted the computer. He wrote a figure less than three hundred dollars above the offer from the Hubberts.

"I'm only doing this to help you out, and because I see they live close enough to get their service from us. Close them now!" Jake glared.

Shamus came back and showed the Hubberts. "Here's the absolute best price you can get on this car. I just need you to sign here, and we can set up delivery." Shamus used an unfeigned "you won" tone of voice.

"I don't believe this," Maisy said.

"No good," Doug said. "Told you what it would take."

"Doug, let's go to Marlo before it gets too late and see if they want to sell us a car." Maisy stood up. Pretzel crumbs and salt showered off her dress.

"Shamus, you had your chance. Bring my money back. We're leaving. If they can't beat your deal, we might come back," Doug said.

"Marlo Honda won't be able to beat this deal. If you think you're going to get big savings from the same car, I think you're in for a surprise."

"We'll see, won't we? Go get my deposit back right now!" Doug raised his voice.

"No need to get angry, Doug. We're trying to work for you, but if you'd feel better shopping around, that's understandable." A cold fury replaced Shamus's earlier flush.

He remained calm and explained to Jake, who could see the pair as they got up.

"All right, let 'em go. I saw you tried, but we can't do better. Follow up, but I know Marlo's going to snap them up just to piss me off."

Shamus handed Doug the hundred and his card.

"Call me if they can't match our price. We can reserve the car over the phone with a credit card. We're here until five today," Shamus said. Maisy walked out without a word.

"I'll let you know either way," Doug said. "If they beat your deal, then you'll know better next time not to jerk your customers around." Doug didn't shake his hand.

Shamus only had one other customer that day, and he was dressed like a wino. He pointed to a Civic on the floor and said, "I'll take it." He left a deposit of twenty dollars and filled out a credit application. A typical "credit rat," combing the dealerships seeing if one was desperate enough to lend him money they'd never see again. Shamus decided not to spend that commission in advance. When he got back to his desk, his message light blinked.

"Shamus, I don't want to say I told you so, but I did. It's Doug Hubbert. Maisy and I are looking at our new car. They beat your deal, and by twenty-eight bucks. Better luck next time."

A whole day pissed away over twenty-eight dollars?

He looked down at the buyer's order. Hmmm, what's this? Name, address, phone number, employment information.

He couldn't wait for his day off.

CHAPTER 10

Door to Door

Newark, Delaware, Sunday afternoon

Out-of-staters always pronounced the name of the town like the one in New Jersey, but Shamus had lived here long enough to know it was pronounced "New-ark."

There was her house. Shamus pulled his car around the corner and double-checked the address. It matched the one Flannigan had given him. The Chinese characters on the mailbox reassured him. He didn't know if she wore a fancy silk robe, but at least she wouldn't be a muscle-bound freak like her son. Washed-up has-been…

He was so glad he'd made time to stop by the gag shop. Shamus glanced in the mirror to make sure his mustache was on straight. The blond wig covered all his red hair. For once, his young looks helped, and he yanked the paper tag off the University of Delaware Blue Hens T-shirt. Perfect. He was just another nice college boy off to make the neighborhood near his frat house a better place before a night of boozing and filthy little coeds.

This would provide excellent practice before the festivities tomorrow night. He picked up his clipboard and walked up the path of the neat town house and rapped on the door. Might take a while; she's probably old.

The door popped open before the third knock. An old, thin Chinese guy fixed him with a penetrating look. "Yes?"

Flannigan didn't say anything about a man. Chang's father? Pretty small—Mama-san would have to be a whale given the size of her son…

"Yes?" The old man repeated. Might be his entire English vocabulary.

"Good afternoon, sir. My name is Casey; I'm from UD." Shamus pointed at his shirt.

No response. Eyed him like he was a bug. Don't touch the mustache—it's fine.

Shamus spoke slowly. "My fraternity wants to help with chores for older Newark residents…" Nothing. He might as well have said he was Bluto from Delta House. "Is the lady of the house home?"

"No home. You go."

"Anyone else I can talk to?"

"Nobody home. You go now."

Who'd he think he was? Jumbo-sized cops were one thing; maybe he'd step inside for a little peek, remind this runt of his size. Shamus pulled out a flyer he stole off a windshield earlier.

"Alrighty then, boss, I'll just leave this flyer on the table here…" Shamus brushed past the old prick. He started to extend his arm to drop off the paper.

One of the man's hands moved in a blur. His fingers dug into Shamus's forearm like talons, and pain exploded down to his hand. Shamus saw the paper flutter from his tingling digits.

"Go. Now."

"Goddamn, what did you do?" Shamus used his good hand to shove the old man, who released the arm and pivoted his shoulders. It felt like Shamus had pushed loose canvas.

An instant later, the man stuck one finger under Shamus's chin. Agony flared along his jaw, and he was forced to stand on tiptoes in an effort to reduce the pressure. Shamus hopped backward, but the man kept lifting and walked him away from the door like he was some sort of trained monkey. Shamus fell down, and the old man stood his ground with the same stony expression.

"Go."

Fuck this. Shamus kept the clipboard and managed to get to his feet. His heart pounded. He opened his mouth to say something, he wasn't sure what, but the man shifted his weight toward him and Shamus felt all resolve crumble. He turned and sprinted down the block. His legs felt fine, and he ran past his car before he looked back to see if this crazy bastard was chasing him. No.

Shamus got back to his car, and the shakes set in. He managed to get the car started and the radio turned on full blast before he cut loose with a scream. He could move his fingers, but the pain lingered. His jaw ached, and the scream hurt. He closed his eyes and tried to let the music wash over him, but he heard a familiar voice over the music.

"Scared, scared..."

He changed the station. Country, but it didn't matter.

"Scared little boy..."

Another station. Rap.

Gran's voice was loud and clear now. "Miserable excuse for a boy, let alone a man."

"Shut up!" Shamus pushed in the lighter.

"You know what happens to bad boys…"

The lighter popped out.

"They need the mark of cowardice."

"Yes." Shamus pulled down his pants and slid his boxers up to the last circular scar. Placement was everything, or she'd never stop. He knew she was right.

"What are you waiting for, boy?"

Shamus tugged the lighter free, and the orange coils glowed. He pressed the tip onto his inner thigh. He couldn't hear the hiss, but the smoke hit his nostrils a moment later. The pain washed him clean and pushed aside the bruises from the old man. Gran's presence left the car without a sound. She knew he'd finish the work later and rub ashes into the wound to make the scar permanent, just like she showed him.

He didn't mind. The rules were different now. He knew what to do to make her proud.

CHAPTER 11

Lake Effect

Monday morning

Chang crossed a quiet lake. His paddle left gentle ripples on the water's surface. A noise shook his concentration, and he struggled to preserve the image. The paddle turned into a tennis racket. Tennis balls bobbed up around the canoe like eyes and stared at Chang. *She had green eyes…*

"How many times have I told you not to move your goddamned desk?"

Chang abandoned his meditation and opened his eyes. Sergeant Foley leaned over him. Sausage on his breath. Chang's desk was turned perpendicular to the rest of the neat rows of detective desks. A small electric fountain and wind chime sat on the flat surface.

"The same number of times I've told you I need the desk facing *that* wall so I can align my qi."

"I don't know what you're talking about, and I don't give a rat's ass about your kee! Your spiritual guru ain't in charge of this room, I am." Foley's uniform looked like it had been starched while he wore it.

Chang stood and eyed the vulnerable points on Foley's body. So easy, one quick strike... The Dragon's heartbeat quickened his own pulse.

"It better be straight when I get back." Foley left.

Chang remained still and allowed his blood pressure to drop. He wasn't sure which relaxed him more, the feng shui or the fact that it annoyed Foley.

Nelson walked in and must have caught the end of the exchange. "Ever hear the one about 'the nail that sticks up gets pounded down'?"

Chang waved the idea away. "He won't make it physical. Fear rules Foley, and I can control myself."

Nelson looked unconvinced.

"Ed Wiggins just came by."

"Really?" Chang feigned surprise.

"Apologized and everything. I hope you didn't threaten *him.*" Nelson met his eyes. Scanned him.

"I wouldn't do that."

"You might."

"Well I *didn't.*" Chang yanked back the angry red mist that tried to drift from Foley toward Nelson. "I let them know what happened and that you're a hell of cop."

Nelson stared at the floor. "Was."

"*Are*—it's part of your nature. You aren't happy here."

Nelson pulled a notepad from his back pocket. "Nobody is. Look. I staked out the mall across the street for two weeks. More than two-thirds of the people who walked by weren't happy. I read it off them like they carried signs."

Chang hadn't realized how much Nelson missed investigating. "Meet me for lunch today. I need your help."

CHAPTER 12
Off the Bench

Chang showed up on time with a briefcase in one hand and a takeout bag in the other. The weather was cool, in the high fifties, but the sun shone. They walked to the outdoor eating area with half a dozen picnic tables and chose one furthest from any other diners.

"I'll get right to the point." Chang took sandwiches out of the bag. "Do you know about the Vietnamese couple killed in their store a few weeks back?"

"Saw it in the paper. A double. Rare around here."

"Yes, it could be a hit from a shakedown, but I don't think so."

"There's more." Nelson made it a fact, not a question.

"If there weren't, I wouldn't need a wreck like you, would I?" Chang saw the remark had stung. "Sorry. You know I didn't mean that."

"Maybe you're desperate." Nelson flashed a rare smile. "So you think we have a hunter?"

We? Good.

"Maybe. I don't know." Chang knew his frustration showed. He pulled out a folder. "I borrowed the case file."

Nelson reached for the papers. "Let's have a look."

"Not here. You're a civilian. Later."

"I never felt like a cop when I was one. Now I don't feel like a civilian."

"Never mind the file; I want your first instincts."

"I'm rusty, but what else sticks out on these cases?" Nelson spoke around a bite of sandwich.

"The papers left out plenty." Chang lowered his voice and told him about the cans of food and the produce in the laps of the victims.

"Interesting. Both shot in the head, execution style. Money gone. Produce in laps. Both victims clothed?"

"Yes."

"Signs of struggle? Defensive wounds on the hands, anything like that?"

"It looks like they were tied up before the perp got physical." Chang hoped it was quick for them. Escaped the horrors of Vietnam only to get shot in Wilmington.

"Enemies?"

Chang mentioned the payoffs.

"Do gangs use melons for silencers these days?"

"I don't think so. That bothered me. Did you see the news item recently about a convenience store shooting?"

"They quoted you, and you didn't tell the reporter anything. Some 7-Eleven guy shot and robbed, was that it?"

Nelson's memory was never rusty.

"It seemed like a pure vanilla robbery/homicide at first." Chang covered the basic facts and the lemon.

"Broke the nose?"

"The killer was angry about something." Chang couldn't get the citrus smell out of his mind. He wished Nelson could have seen it up close.

"Set off, or was it a grudge?"

"That's not clear. The guns are different, and the Nguyens were shot execution style, and in this case the killer faced his victim. But then there's the fruit."

"Walk me through the facts." Nelson sat perfectly still and closed his eyes.

Chang recited the key points. "Two sets of murders a couple weeks apart. Peel back the surface and both could be anger related. Plus the food element."

"Robbery, crimes took place later at night, the victims were ethnic, two Vietnamese, one Indian." Nelson whispered. He opened his eyes. "No magic yet. I want to see the files."

"We'll put our heads together." Like old times…an unfortunate reason for nostalgia, but there it was.

Chang watched Nelson take out a calendar and flip though blank pages. "I don't have much to do after work this week, except walk Daisy, so I guess we're on." They cleared the table and walked back to the building.

Chang could swear there was a bounce in Nelson's step.

CHAPTER 13

Smoke and Melons

Bear, Monday evening

At the sound of the doorbell, Chang heard Daisy's baying bark. Nelson opened the door, and Chang knelt down and scratched the basset hound's stomach when she rolled over for him.

Chang walked down a narrow hallway to the dining room. He put his briefcase on a green table. The whole town house smelled musty from tall stacks of old books all around.

"Some watchdog." Nelson moved books off the table.

Chang couldn't get past the all–earth-tone-green furniture. "Did you decorate yourself?"

"I like it. That's a quiet color."

Chang felt distracted. He stared at the dining room table.

"What?"

Chang craved order. "This room is out of harmony."

"I know it's a mess, but it's *my* mess." Nelson hovered behind Chang.

Chang tried to ignore the disarray. He didn't have to live here. "Let's get to work."

Nelson opened each file and spread the contents on the dining room table. Harmony or not, Chang felt more relaxed.

Nelson read Chang's report in silence. He picked up the crime scene photographs. He held a close-up picture of a shattered melon with powder burns.

"No wonder nobody heard anything. But did this guy plan to kill them, or was it spur of the moment? Was it just for the money? Their son said they kept a decent amount of cash around, isn't that right?"

"They didn't trust banks. The kid said they would have given a robber money in the register, but their main stash was in a secret hiding place."

"Who knew about it?"

"He did, of course. Maybe the gangs suspected." Chang knew gangs usually didn't kill a "customer" who complied.

Nelson chewed a thumbnail and spoke rapidly. "Someone kills this couple like a pro hit, takes their money, and then dumps groceries in their laps. What's professional about that? Next, robbery of a convenience store, clerk killed, then he gets a lemon smashed into his face after he's dead. With enough force to break the nose. Rational clues, then a curveball." Chang knew Nelson spoke more to himself.

Nelson looked at the photo series from the Patel homicide. He placed the pictures of Patel's face with the lemon alongside each other. Chang could hear a soft whistle from Nelson's nose when he breathed.

"The robbery is smoke. Both robberies are smoke." Nelson stared at the photos. "This is rage." He pointed at Patel. "And so is this." He tapped the shot of the dead Vietnamese couple. "It's harder to tell with the first, but the produce is the anger. Why a lemon and not a melon?" Nelson looked up. Chang mentioned his idea about lemongrass and Vietnamese cuisine.

"This kind of fury burns like a fire. It gets bigger before it goes out. I hope we're both wrong."

Chang knew they weren't. "So what do we do about it?"

Nelson shrugged. "I guess we follow our nature."

"Welcome back, Flash." Chang hadn't used that nickname in years.

CHAPTER 14

All in the Delivery

Greenville, Delaware, Monday morning

Shamus wished for the first time in a while that he didn't have to go in to the dealership. He was anxious to work on his next project.

After the encounter with that vicious little praying mantis at Chang's mother's house yesterday, Shamus couldn't wait to rebound. He reviewed every facet of his plan. Not as simple as Patel, but worth the extra effort. If Patel was a "quickie," this time he would savor a nice, long session. Those two slugs deserved what was coming. When he'd felt the calm wash over him Saturday, he knew Gran had sent these Takers to him for a reason.

He'd sold his ass off on Saturday, and nothing was good enough for these pigs.

After the weekend's sales debacle Tommy was going to be difficult to catch, but Shamus knew he could still do it.

Shamus rolled into the dealership for the Monday staff meeting with the owner, Fred Baer, who owned several other car franchises in addition to the Honda dealership. These meetings bored Shamus; they were usually reviews of generic car-selling techniques. Beginner stuff. Baer may have been a successful businessman, but Shamus could teach him a thing or two about public speaking. He wasn't a people person like Shamus.

In the meeting room, Jonah sat next to him.

"Hi, Jonah, good weekend?"

"Can't complain. Got lots of sleep and recharged the batteries. Hey, tough break with those guys on Saturday."

"Already forgotten. Onward and upward, right?" Shamus gave him a big grin. "Way to go with your customers. I saw they bought, finally."

"Oh, yeah. Finally is right. They about wore me out. Mrs. Chen was a hammer. Mr. Chen spoke no English. It took me the whole day to close them, but I'll be glad when they're over the curb," Jonah said.

Learn from his patience.

The rest of the team filed in, and the meeting started. Shamus tuned out as soon as he heard the topic: "How to fill out a buyer's order correctly."

Early this morning Shamus had done a dry run to the Hubberts' development. They lived in North Wilmington just off Route 202. He drove past their house, unconcerned that he used his own car. He would borrow another vehicle tonight. No more winging it after yesterday. The burn on his leg reminded him of the price of failure.

He'd seen the Hubberts' new car in the driveway. The white temporary tag mocked him. He hoped they were enjoying it. They weren't going to have to worry about how long the new-car smell would last.

Among the props from Sunday's little shopping spree he'd picked up some handcuffs. Not police grade, but they'd do the job. At least nobody at the novelty shop asked questions. At a hardware store he bought more duct tape. Great stuff. Easy to use, let him get control quickly. His last stop was a bakery to pick up a loaf of French bread from the day-old basket. He could almost smell the wonderful aroma from that little shop when the end of the meeting broke into his reverie.

"So remember, everyone, when you fill out the buyer's order properly the first time, you save time. Got it? First time, save time, means more time for sales." Baer nodded as if he'd just dispensed the wisdom of the ages.

Jake clapped his hands loudly:

"Well, let's get 'em. Let's get another week off to a good start. You guys are doing a great job; don't let up," Jake said.

Shamus only forgot about the Hubberts when he was busy with a delivery to some pleasant customers. The day dragged on.

By early evening he'd collected a couple of good prospects, and just after dinner he sold a Civic to a nice Korean woman who was looking for a car for her son.

"Okay, Mrs. Kim, if we get you this price," Shamus said, pointing to her offer, which actually allowed the dealership and him to make a profit, "and I give you first oil change free, we have deal?" He found he lapsed into broken English, but he wasn't trying to patronize her.

"Well, maybe I think about it," she said, but she made no move to leave. Shamus knew it was time to close the deal.

"Two oil changes, a free carwash…and this." He held up the plastic pen with the dealership logo. Sold.

Why couldn't all customers be like the Johnsons or Mrs. Kim? Here's a nice car, here's a good deal, you give me some money, here are the keys, have a nice life.

Dale Olinger, the burly finance manager and self-described "dirty old man," had dropped by his cubicle earlier that day with the credit report on that rat from last Saturday, his one big "sale" for that miserable day.

"Tell your customer that if he wants a loan he doesn't need to pay all his bills, but it would help if he occasionally paid one or two," Dale said.

Shamus shrugged.

"Nice job today." Jake told him before they closed the store. "Way to bounce back after a tough Saturday."

"Hey, have a nice day off, Shamus." Jonah rolled out the door. By five minutes past nine the place was nearly empty. Shamus knew he couldn't just wait around. He'd swiped the spare key to a Camry earlier. He'd come back for it when the coast was clear.

Shamus smirked at the warning sign below the dummy security camera. He was glad the owners were too cheap to pay for the real thing.

Shamus drove off and cruised around for thirty minutes. He felt the tension build. Once he thought enough time had passed, he returned to the dealership.

The place was dark inside and quiet outside. He moved past the front of the building and parked near the back of the lot by the Camry. He unloaded his supplies into the black car, and then moved his car a block away, near a local bar.

The Toyota carried him toward his quarry. Fairbridge, the Hubberts' development. He saw one old man walking a dog; neither appeared to take notice. When Shamus turned onto the Hubberts' street, he pulled a baseball cap low onto his head. He rolled past the house and saw a couple lights downstairs and the telltale bluish flicker of a TV set from what had to be a bedroom.

He parked just past their driveway and got out of the car with his grocery bag of goodies. The loaf of French bread stuck out the top. He marched up the front walkway and knocked on the door. The Hubberts didn't have a peep-hole. They'd have to open the door to see who was there. His heart raced when the porch light snapped on. He heard first one lock and then a second click, and the door opened to reveal Maisy in all her house-coated glory.

CHAPTER 15

Crunch Time

Shamus held up the bag to obscure his face and stepped close. "Sorry I'm late. Here are the groceries you ordered. That'll be thirty-eight dollars and sixteen cents."

"What? We didn't order anything. You have the wrong house." Maisy started to close the door.

"Doug said you were hungry and to come quickly. Ask him, he's right behind you." Doug's name gave Shamus the moment he needed.

Maisy looked confused and turned. Her head snapped back to the door, but Shamus stepped into the opening and pointed a pistol inches from her nose.

"Not a sound. Not if you want to live. I just want money and I'll be gone."

Maisy's mouth opened and closed like a bass out of water. Shamus nudged her backwards and stepped into the hallway. He closed the door.

He heard movement from upstairs and glanced up. He spun Maisy around and whispered, "Move!" He walked her toward the kitchen, away from the landing of the stairs.

"Maise? Who was that?" Doug called downstairs.

A pet name. How sweet.

"Not one word, 'Maze,' or I'll take you both out." Shamus spotted a telephone mounted on the wall and put down the grocery bag on the kitchen table. He picked up the phone, heard a dial tone, and left it off the hook.

"Maise?" Doug called again. Maisy whimpered.

"Don't get cute. His life is in your hands." Shamus stood behind her.

He put one hand on her shoulder and guided her to sit at the kitchen table. He made sure she could feel the cold steel of the revolver on her neck.

"Tell him you can't hear him and to come downstairs. If you warn him, I'll shoot you both. Do this right and I'm gone in five minutes."

"I, I can't hear you," Maisy yelled feebly upstairs. "Come here."

Doug's voice carried down the stairs. "Who was at the door, Maise?"

Shamus grabbed her hair and pressed the barrel to the side of her head.

Nasty, greasy stuff.

"Get down here, Doug!" she yelped.

Too loud!

His finger began to tighten on the trigger until he heard Doug's irritation.

"Christ, Maise! What's your problem?" The heavy sound of his tread came down the steps.

"Say nothing," Shamus hissed.

Doug walked down the hallway and turned into the kitchen. He wore baggy pajama bottoms without a shirt to conceal his flabby chest and stomach. His indignant tone vanished when he saw Maisy with a gun to her head.

What a Kodak moment!

"Wha—?" He stopped short, and a ripple of flesh continued forward.

"Hi, Doug!" Shamus felt control return. "Listen up. No heroics, just do what I say and you guys are going to be fine. If you run or try anything, you're going to get Maze here shot, then yourself. Sound good?" Shamus gave him his best Patriot Motors smile.

"Wha…?"

"Doug, focus. You need to be quick on the uptake like your best girl. She understands that if you go along you'll get another chance to drive that new car. Keep gobbling like that, you'll make me jumpy."

Too fun.

"Okay, take two baby steps forward and put on what I give you. No screaming, no talking, nothing sudden, just relax and do it." Shamus reached one hand into the bag. He kept the gun pointed at Doug.

"Why?" Doug seemed to recognize Shamus.

Shamus kept his voice calm and raised the pistol to Maisy's head. "Shut up. You're making me nervous now; keep it up and bad things are going to happen fast."

Doug closed his mouth. Shamus pulled out two pairs of handcuffs. He handed them both to Maisy.

"Doug, walk slowly forward, and then, Maisy, you put one set of these on his wrists, then onto yourself."

"Why?" Doug said again.

Pig. Shamus clubbed Doug on the collarbone with the butt of the gun and aimed at his face. The fat man yelped.

"Put them on!" Animals still loose. Shamus's heart pounded.

A minute later both Doug and Maisy were in cuffs. Better.

"That wasn't so hard, was it? Now, downstairs to the basement where you won't be in my way." Shamus could see doubt on Doug's face.

This guy was such a pain in the ass.

"Here's the deal. I want you out of sight and quiet so I can get the money you owe me for all my trouble on Saturday. Can't do that if I think you're going to try something or call the cops, can I?"

Now they took him seriously.

"Maisy, get up. Doug, you first, then her. Downstairs and not a word."

They both walked to the basement door, and Doug managed to open it. Shamus didn't know what was down there, but Doug couldn't grab a weapon with cuffs on. Other than Maisy crying, which Shamus didn't mind, they stayed quiet.

The basement was unfinished, with a concrete floor and walls. At one end a washer and dryer, at the other a heavy worktable and a pegboard with tools hanging from it. A pipe ran from the floor up through the ceiling. A portable card table and folding chairs leaned against another wall.

Shamus placed the grocery bag on the floor. He took a small set of keys and tossed them to Doug. They smacked into his stomach and dropped to the floor.

"Pick up the keys, open your cuffs, and lock your leg to the leg of that table, above the crossbar, nice and secure."

Doug managed, though Shamus saw the fat man's hands were shaking.

"Throw the keys back. There you go." Shamus smiled again. "Now, Maisy, take these. Lock yourself to that pipe." She cuffed her wrist.

Shamus grabbed two folding chairs and gave one to each.

"There. Much better!" Shamus tucked the pistol into his belt.

"What do you want, Shamus?" Doug called him by name for the first time.

"Hey, you remember me! I'm touched. I told you upstairs that I wanted money."

"Take the money, we have a little here, just don't hurt us. I have a couple hundred upstairs and some jewelry."

"Ah, ah. How can we possibly negotiate on an empty stomach? Maisy here must be starving, aren't you?"

"No, please let us go."

"Oh come now, you can't tell me with all this excitement you aren't feeling at least a little peckish? No? Don't be coy. What sort of guest would I be if I didn't bring something for the hosts?"

He reached into the bag, pulled out a loaf of French bread, and waved it like a baton.

"Shamus, please. Take our money and go. Take it and we won't say anything, I promise. You can have the new car if you want," Doug said.

Shamus looked at Doug at the mention of the car. He walked over to Maisy. "Ah, yes, the new car. How much did you save again? You remember don't you, Maze?"

"No." Her voice quavered.

"I don't think that's true." He put the bread in her lap and took out a roll of duct tape. He took her free arm and wound tape around both until they were trapped together.

"What are you doing to her?" Doug sounded frantic.

"Stop your whining. If you really want me to leave, you're going to have to earn it. Make it worth my while." He grinned.

"What do you mean?" Doug spoke in a stammer.

"We're going to play a game, and if you win, I leave."

"I thought you wanted money."

"Oh, Douglas. Man does not live by bread alone, sometimes he needs a Diet Pepsi to wash it down with, right, Maze?" He bopped her on the head with the loaf of bread, and crumbs showered down her hair. She let out a screech.

"Hush." Shamus took a strip of tape and placed it over her mouth. Her nose made a wet rattle when she breathed.

Lovely.

"Saturday, I wanted money. I guess you did too because you sold me out to those pricks at Marlo for twenty-eight bucks!" Shamus could feel the blood sing in his ears. Felt good.

No. It felt fucking great!

"You said I had my chance, but I blew it. Well, here's your chance, Dougie, and I'm raising the stakes."

Doug's face went slack. "Are you crazy?"

"That's not your problem right now. Your only concern is to do what you do best." Shamus pulled out a pair of party-size bags of Nacho Cheese Doritos.

"All you need to do is finish both bags in two minutes and I'll be on my way. You wasted my time, and this is my way of returning the favor. No big deal, right?"

"You *are* crazy. You can't do this."

"Missing the big picture here. What I *am* is in charge, and don't forget it. I can do anything I want, and what I want right now is to see if you can win this little challenge. You want me to leave, right? That's what it will take."

"What if I say no?" Doug spoke in a timid whisper.

"Oh, hey, this is America, of course. You can always refuse. You'll have to watch Maze here suffocate, but you do have a choice. What'll it be, sport?"

Maisy began to struggle, but Shamus rapped her several times with the bread.

"Stop that, you. Us menfolk are talking. What do you say, Doug? Might be your house, but they're my rules, and you don't have long to decide." Shamus opened the two bags and placed them on the table in front of Doug, who had the use of his hands.

"Up to you, but the two minutes start in three, two, one, *go!*" Shamus consulted his watch. Doug grabbed chips by the fistful and shoveled them into his mouth.

"Crunch all you want; I have more."

Not bad. Was he going to make it?

Early into the second bag, Doug ran into trouble. With about forty seconds to go, he lapsed into a violent coughing fit. Chip fragments spewed from his mouth in a cloud. Maisy squirmed. Shamus was glad of the tape over her mouth, because it sounded like she was trying to make some serious noise.

Twenty seconds to go. He'd never make it. What a shame. He decided to let Doug play out the clock, in the spirit of sportsmanship.

"Time's up. I'm sorry. What a great effort from our champion, but it looks like he choked at the end. Too bad." Shamus didn't try to hide his glee. He walked over to Maisy. Doug still gasped. Her nose began to honk with increased demand for air.

Shamus clamped a piece of the sturdy tape over both piggy little nostrils. Her struggles grew frantic.

Wow! Shamus stepped back to watch.

Doug roared and managed to grab a hammer from his pegboard. The table slid across the floor with each lunge like a ball and chain. His face was smeared with bright orange flavoring from the chips.

"You look like a bad clown!" Shamus avoided the charge and danced around, just out of reach. He laughed and taunted him. Maisy's thrashing subsided. Doug looked exhausted, but he threw the hammer at Shamus's head. Shamus saw it and got his arms up just in time. The hammer struck his left elbow on the "funny bone" with a shock that ran up the nerve. His arm went numb, followed by an excruciating burning sensation.

Bastard!

Rage clouded Shamus's vision. He picked up the hammer and felt the first connection with Doug's head. Doug fell silent, though Shamus paid no attention and swung the hammer again, again, again.

He snapped out of his frenzy and looked down. Gore covered the hammer and his right arm halfway up to the elbow. His clothes looked as if they'd been spray painted red.

Maisy's body lay crumpled at the bottom of the pipe where she'd collapsed. Shamus dropped the hammer in his paper bag and pulled the tape off her mouth. He tossed the piece aside. No more honks. Shamus took the loaf of French bread and stuck one end in her mouth and pushed it in as far as he could. She looked better now.

He stripped off his shirt and stuffed it into the paper bag. The pants and shoes weren't too bad, so he left them on and walked upstairs. He turned out the lights and made his way to the second-floor bedroom. He went to the bathroom and washed most of the blood off his hands and arm. He grabbed a large shirt out of the walk-in closet. Of course it didn't fit, but he put it on anyway. The television continued to gab, and he turned off an infomercial on how to lose weight without exercise.

He headed down the stairs and noticed he'd tracked some blood on the way up. He checked the soles of his shoes. Clean enough. No big deal, as long as he didn't mess up the borrowed car. He wasn't going to keep the shoes, anyway.

He went back down to the basement, snapped on the light, and took one more look at what his power had created. After he got home, it would be hours before he could sleep.

CHAPTER 16

Back in the Game

Wilmington, Tuesday morning

Nelson picked up right away, and Chang felt his shoulders unknot.

"I need you to get back up to Wilmington as fast as you can."

"I just got to Dover. What is it?"

"Another double. Bad. You need to see this."

"Where are you?"

"Off 202 in North Wilmington. Keep this quiet. We got the call half an hour ago. One of the victims is in a carpool. The driver knocked and then went through the unlocked back door. She found the victims in the basement." Chang wanted to get Nelson in before the ME removed the bodies.

"Can you describe the scene to me?"

"Not over the phone. Can you come?"

"On my way."

Chang watched a beat-up car circle the block for the second time, and he walked toward it. He memorized the license plate, but the car pulled to the curb and the driver's door opened. Chang unbuttoned his jacket to clear his holster.

At first Chang thought the man was crouching, but when he saw the white hair and bent frame he recognized the reporter. Chang never met him, but the wizened figure was a legend at the *Daily Post.* He could almost see the man's troubles weigh on his stooped shoulders. Chang had his own concerns. Besides, what was he doing here?

"You must be Flannigan."

"You must be Chang."

"Our reputations precede us. Something I can do for you?"

"Sure. Mind if I take a look inside?" His body tilted back so he could look Chang in the face.

"Of course I mind. Why are you here?"

"Cover a story. Some detective." Flannigan began to cough. He lit a cigarette. "Another double homicide. Do you think it's a pattern?"

"That isn't on the wire. How'd you hear about it?" Chang stared at the man and tried to imagine him involved in the crime. He looked like he'd barely be able to lift a melon, let alone kill anyone.

"I'll take that as a confirmation."

"Once more. How did you know this was a murder scene?"

"I told you. I'm a reporter. I got sources." Flannigan shuffled to the edge of the crime scene line.

Someone was going to pay for that leak. He knew this Flannigan was an un-lanced boil, but no killer. His mind returned to the scene inside the house.

* * *

Nelson must have pushed his rattletrap car to the limit because he arrived in just thirty minutes. Chang met him at the yellow tape and logged him in under his authority. He pointed out Flannigan to the officers. "You don't want to see me again if he gets past you."

The rookie looked ready to shoot the old man if he crossed the line. No doubt one of the veterans had whispered rumors about Chang into his ear. He didn't care as long as Flannigan didn't get through.

Chang carried a pair of paper suits complete with booties over his arm. Nelson ducked under the yellow tape, and Chang handed an outfit to him. He put his on.

"Are they okay with me here? Hey, you remembered my size." Nelson donned the suit and began to sweat.

"This is my crime scene. They don't have a choice." It was a temporary solution. The brass would pitch a fit, but he needed to preserve his serenity for the task at hand. He'd worry about them later.

Chang let Nelson look at the front door and watched his old partner's gaze trace the area around the lock. Same thing Chang did earlier. The two stepped inside, and Nelson went to work.

Chang could smell stale fried chicken and onion rings. He pointed to the dried, bloody footprints that led to the staircase and upstairs. It was the right foot, and the prints got fainter up the stairs. Nelson made a note of it in a small, spiral-bound notebook and avoided the prints that emerged from the basement door.

"Let's go downstairs. The coroner estimated time of death as last night, probably before midnight." How long could he keep Nelson on the scene?

When they reached the stairs, the odors hit Chang all over again. Death had a distinct reek, one never forgotten. The brine-over-pennies smell of blood, heavy in the close basement, would take Nelson right back to detective mode.

The wooden steps creaked under their weight. The limited view of the basement floor expanded, and Chang saw the edges of a large pool of blood, the first sneaker print pointing away from it. They reached the landing.

About six feet from the bottom of the stairs, surrounded by the blood, lay a large shirtless man in pajama bottoms. The gore came from his shattered head. A visual ID based on the face alone would be tricky; luckily the hands were intact.

The top of the head was completely collapsed, and Chang could make out a couple places where there was a distinct circular shape to the wounds that penetrated the skull. Chang tried to imagine what could drive someone to this level of fury.

Nelson spoke aloud to himself. “Hammer. Got to be.”

A second body lay slumped at the base of a pipe. A large woman handcuffed and taped to the pipe. Her cause of death was less readily apparent. Chang stared at the long loaf of bread that stuck out of her mouth.

The sight and smells of bodies, the voided bladders and emptied bowels all came with the job. Death he understood. Anger too. Even fiery rage that clawed for an outlet. Despite the silence, this room carried the shriek of insanity. His mind skipped to a slim young girl in a tennis dress dumped on a tennis court. Jennifer Topper. Green eyes…the texture of felt…

Chang dragged his thoughts back to the present and tried to absorb the import of what he saw. The pair of bright orange Doritos bags caught his gaze. More food. He noticed the crumbs all over the floor and saw the bits of orange powder mixed with the blood on what remained of the male victim's face.

Chang pointed to the floor. "Check it out." The scrape marks from the legs of the workbench showed it had moved from under a pegboard with tools. The guy had dragged the bench by his handcuffed leg.

"You fought. Good for you," Nelson said. "Did you get him, too?"

Chang looked for another source of blood spatters but saw none. He began to feel anger simmer. The order of the tools brought home the sense that these were regular folks. They weren't dope pushers or gang bangers. What could the victims have possibly done that would warrant this degrading execution? Chang tried to picture snowy mountains but came up with a volcano.

Nelson tugged Chang out of the way. "You're jamming me." Chang knew that when he got upset, Nelson picked up on it. He moved back and watched his partner. Nelson held up his hands to make a frame with his fingers and looked at the room a section at a time. Chang still needed a camera.

"What's this?" Nelson pointed to a strip of duct tape near the corner on the floor. It matched the tape on the female victim.

Nelson rocked his body forward and back, forward and back. He made a low noise that sounded like a hum, but Chang knew it was a phrase repeated rapid-fire. Something he did when he wanted to block out the rest of the world.

Nelson stopped rocking and spoke to her still form. "You were already dead before he did that bit with the French bread, weren't you? Why'd you let him in? Did you know him? Were you friends? Why did you give him control and then fight later? Help me out."

Nelson took another look and whispered to Chang, "Were they out of lemons?"

Nelson's quip felt like an icicle in Chang's gut. He already knew these weren't random acts.

They walked back to the first floor. Chang saw that Nelson's hands shook.

Nelson gestured to the second floor. "You go upstairs yet?"

"Just to make sure there weren't any other victims."

Nelson went up the stairs. "C'mon."

Chang saw by the footprints that the killer had only gone into the master bedroom. They stepped around the prints and saw the tidy room. The bed was made, but it appeared by the arrangement of the pillows and the single impression on the bedspread that one person had probably been watching television. Given the man's state of dress, more than likely the wife either let the killer in or was overpowered.

Chang saw the traces of blood on the floor leading into the bathroom and noted a faint crimson hue in the sink.

Nelson whispered, "Washed your hands."

"He picked out a new shirt, too." Chang saw reddish smudges leading to the closet. The neat row of shirts on hangers was disturbed by one empty hanger with a bent hook on the floor. The rest of the closet looked tidier than most clothes shops.

"There's something else." Chang pointed to the dresser where a man's watch and a money clip filled with bills sat in plain sight.

"Bingo!" Nelson looked over to the wife's dresser. Chang could see several rings and a gold necklace.

"He forgot to steal anything, maybe too excited." Chang felt a surge of satisfaction.

"You probably need to get me out of here."

Chang became aware of the passage of time and the increased number of vehicles outside. Nelson had to be gone before more media showed up.

"Yes. I might be able to clear out in a couple of hours, at least for a break. Can you meet me somewhere?"

"Sure."

"There's a snack shop over in Independence Mall on 202, about a mile from here. The place is called Tea Hee. Two hours?"

"I know the spot. I'll see you at noon. Call if you won't make it." Nelson started toward his car.

"Nelson."

"What?"

Chang pointed.

"You might want to take that off." Chang removed his own paper suit and accepted Nelson's. "Don't talk to that short guy stalking the line. He's press, not a friend."

"Not talking to people is my specialty."

CHAPTER 17
Tea for Two

A couple of hours later, Chang pulled into the shopping center, an exact replica of Independence Hall in Philadelphia.

Inside there was a small line, and he spotted Nelson already seated. Chang could see Nelson drawing salt doodles on the table. After rough crime scenes he'd be apt to empty a shaker and trace patterns in the pile of crystals. Chang told him he would order first. The girl behind the counter had a pierced nose and enough earrings to set off a metal detector.

He paid the cashier and joined Nelson.

"Did you get the chai? I hear it's great." Chang took a seat.

"I'll have to try it sometime."

Chang looked at him for a moment and then asked, "Earl Grey?" Nelson tended to lose composure in front of strangers and only remember what he didn't want. "You were cool around dead bodies, but can't handle the pressure of a simple order?"

"Long line, too many choices..." Nelson looked up from his salt art. "This is a hunter."

"I think so too. What's with the food? Produce, lemons, bread, and chips? I don't get it, but whoever this is he's getting worse." Explosive violence, intensely personal.

"Mr. Three Percent!" the counter girl called out.

"I think that's me," Nelson said.

Chang watched Nelson shuffle back with his tea like it was an unstable explosive. He didn't spill a drop and set the cup aside.

"Three percent?"

"I told the woman at the counter that with all the metal in her head she was three percent more likely to get hit by lightning." Nelson looked back at her. "She doesn't like me."

"Just hope she didn't spit in it."

Nelson smoothed the salt into a thin pile. "The thefts from the first two times were cover. He was so hyped last night he forgot to steal anything. He got up close and personal. The Nguyens were close, but he shot them from behind. Must not have wanted to look in their eyes."

"First-time jitters?"

"Yes. The melon was from the store. He didn't plan to kill them. Not consciously."

"How so?" This was new. Chang envied the way Nelson could wrap a killer's mind around himself.

"I don't know him well yet, but he did too much planning to get the Nguyens vulnerable only to rob them. Deep down, he knew he'd kill but had to talk himself into it."

New to killing?

"The second one was face to face," Chang said, "but quick, and he used a gun. He did the lemon afterwards, when the victim couldn't fight back."

"Yes. When he killed the Hubberts he had them under control like the first time, but the violence was more personal. Got his hands dirty."

"He took a shirt. Do you think the killings didn't go the way he'd planned?" Chang sipped his ginseng tea. Not bad, but next time he'd bring Shu's fresh blend and order hot water.

"Doug fought."

"Yes, I thought maybe he was trying to get away and the killer caught him." Chang watched Nelson close his eyes. He could see them move under the lids like the REM of a dreamer.

"All the tools in their place but one. The hammer, at the bottom, in reach of someone locked to that table. Doug tried to fight. Got the hammer. Only made our guy mad." Nelson recited the images that Chang knew flickered across his mind.

"What about the wife and the bread?" Chang didn't want to interrupt, but he was too curious.

Nelson opened his eyes. "I don't know, but it's postmortem, like the lemon."

Chang pictured the scene and voiced his thought. "The piece of tape on the floor…maybe that's what set off the husband. Is this guy sick enough to make his victim watch his own wife suffocate?"

"If not, he will be soon." Nelson sipped his tea and grimaced.

"Now, what was his point with corn chips? A failed attempt to choke him? Then he used the bread to make the point on the wife? The stomach contents from the autopsy might shed some light."

Chang drew on a napkin to create a chart for connections and gave up. "A Vietnamese couple, single Indian, white couple. Two killed in their business, one couple in their home. Three victim sets from different cultural backgrounds. The perp knew them all. He had to. They let him get close. That's the key." He took a deep breath. "We already know enough to ask the real question."

Nelson stared out the front window. "Who's next?"

CHAPTER 18

Press On

Greenville, Friday morning

Shamus continued to bask in the afterglow of the previous Monday night. He rose early to work on his "scrapbook," the large corkboard on his bedroom wall. The number of articles climbed. The "Senseless Slaying in the Suburbs" piece was good. His favorite was the latest "Blarney Stone." He chose well.

He took his copy of the *Daily Post* and placed it next to Gran's picture. Gran Ryan's fiery red hair contrasted with her cold blue eyes. He went to the freezer and removed her cremated remains. Water condensed on the chilled exterior of the urn. He read aloud from the article. She would be so proud of him.

Blind Blues?
By Patrick Flannigan

Does Wilmington have its own "Jack the Ripper"? The latest string of murders in our fair city may not be the unfortunate series of random events Police Colonel Byrd would have us believe. Sources close to the "Blarney Stone" reveal the killings may only be the beginning.

Why is the state so reluctant to address the possibility? Repeated calls to headquarters were not returned by time of press, and this reporter spoke directly to the lead investigator, Paul Chang, who refused comment. While we're glad to see that the rank and file so readily follows orders, we have to ask if the citizens don't deserve more.

We don't want to start a panic, but if the very department sworn to serve and protect can't even detect a problem, how will they hope to solve it?

Stick with the Stone, readers. It might be a bumpy ride.

Shamus got the giggles but finished the piece. What a marvelous start. He loved the dig on that oaf Chang. When Gran sent him another Taker, he would feed this Flannigan a bigger taste of the larger design.

Shamus put the urn back in the freezer. His elbow still hurt, but he took the pain like a man and bore the injury as a silent badge to his courage in combat. He'd bested the man of the house and had the scars to prove it.

After the story had broken, at work he thought he was in trouble when Hank dropped a copy of the paper on his desk. The article on the murders showed a color picture of the dearly departed heavies. All smiles in the shot, not so in the end…

"Hey, man, aren't these your people?" Hank had stabbed his finger at the picture.

"My God. You're right. I thought the name sounded familiar, but these folks didn't buy from me." Shamus looked out the showroom window for police cruisers.

"Small town, man. Looks like you can cross them off your follow-up list."

"Hank, that's not funny." Yes it was!

Shamus could laugh all he wanted at home, but he was going to have to be careful around people. Remember, the Hubberts were a hard-working couple who didn't deserve...couldn't even finish the thought. Next time, think of Gran.

Once he knew he was in the clear, he caught fire all week. Not only had he logged three sales so far, with Saturday still ahead, but he had at least three more that showed promise, including the nice older lady who made the porcelain vases for a living. He knew he was going to have to romance Myrtle Maynard to sell her that minivan.

He thought also of Rick Midori, the nervous ferret of a man interested in Honda's most environmentally friendly offerings. The guy especially wanted to know about their hybrid cars, the ones that ran on gas and got an acceleration boost from an electric motor.

But when Shamus had approached him, Midori practically put up a brick wall. His beady eyes darted around, and he had a disgusting layer of sweat on his upper lip.

"I'm merely looking. I work in sales, and don't you worry. If I consummate a transaction from this establishment, you will receive full credit. I'm well acquainted with this industry's compensation structure. Rest assured. Your commission is secure with me."

Did he want to buy a car or screw it?

While they test drove an Insight, Shamus clamped onto the armrest and waited for a chance to get in a word. Midori had droned on about where he worked, what he did, where he'd gone to school, and detailed his membership in the chess club in high school. Normally he could tune out a babbling customer. Midori demanded interaction.

"I'm sorry, do you know what 'punctiliousness' means? Don't be embarrassed. We all can grow." Midori had handed Shamus a pocket dictionary and insisted he look it up. Shamus pretended to do so and fought down the urge to find out how well Midori could drive with the little book crammed down his throat. That had led to a thought about Maisy and a new struggle to hold back the giggles.

Midori was supposed to come back tonight, and Shamus couldn't wait to close Mr. Punctilious. He knew Jake had prepared some strong numbers to wrap it up.

Shamus switched on the radio and caught the last of a news item on the Hubberts. Cool! Have to listen again at the top of the hour. It made him tingle all over because the media coverage had picked up on his extracurricular activities.

He wasn't worried. He knew the police couldn't use much of what they might find, since he had no record. Not here, not in Ohio, not anywhere. No fingerprints, never arrested, not even a speeding ticket.

Gran never wanted to share her control when she was alive. Now she wanted to work with him! He had to admit they made a good team.

Shamus was struck by some of the television interviews of the Hubberts' neighbors. One of them actually said they "couldn't imagine why someone would do such a thing to people like the Hubberts."

Shamus couldn't imagine why someone hadn't done something like this to those cud-chewers before. He didn't expect the greater public to understand. No thanks were necessary.

He pinned up another article, this one from the much less prestigious *Community Events,* but it included a quote from Chang. He gave out a number to call in case anyone had information. Must mean they didn't have any leads. Good.

His elbow ached when he placed the article high up on the corkboard. It hurt less when Shamus pictured how much more the hammer did to Doug. He would have liked to keep the tool for a trophy, but that was a bad idea. He wore gloves, but it didn't make sense to leave a key item like that around. Just in case. Likewise, he made a large collage out of lingerie models from Victoria's Secret catalogs on a piece of white cardboard to cover his newspaper articles.

He shivered when he thought about how long Gran would have made him sit in the old icehouse if she ever saw these dirty girls. She'd have left him on the ice cake in his underwear for at least an hour to "cool his spirits." To this day, whenever a customer yelled at him he could feel the wet sawdust on the back of his legs.

Not to worry. From her vantage point in the freezer she wouldn't get a glimpse of the ladies, even when he went for late-night ice cream.

On Tuesday, Shamus placed all the clothing he'd worn to the Hubberts' house in a paper bag and drove to an old apartment building in Wilmington that still used an incinerator.

On the way back he took the hammer (which wouldn't burn and might be discovered), and in a moment of inspiration he threw it over the fence and into the reservoir for Wilmington. Let the whole city get a little taste of his power!

Shamus tacked up the collage of his "girlfriends" and got dressed. He was working the one o'clock to closing shift.

He remembered that Rick Midori worked somewhere close by. Midori was an antiques and estate appraiser. He established the value of personal property such as furniture and old china and silver. The office was in Greenville and not far from where Shamus lived. Given the Chateau Country further up Route 52, the office was probably in the right place. Shamus hoped to spot something that would help him bond with Midori.

He eyed the address on the wall and followed the lane until he saw the wooden sign for Felton Appraisal Services. Then he saw something else that stopped him cold. There, a few rows over, was a shiny Honda Insight in Navy Blue Pearl.

He couldn't see the back where the license plate would be visible. He felt his pulse start to race in his throat and cruised past then looped back to the next row of parked cars. He slowed and his trained eye picked out the paper temporary tag. He saw from the expiration date it had been purchased yesterday, and the bracket advertised Marlo. His temples began to ache.

He exited the shopping center and aimed his old Accord down Route 52 toward Wilmington. He wouldn't be able to sell anything until he got the answer to his question.

At the dealership, he grabbed Midori's info folder and dialed the work number. "Felton Appraisals, Will Felton speaking."

"Yes, hello. I have a client with a considerable amount of family silver that will be going to probate, and he would like an accurate estimation of its value." Shamus hoped he sounded like an attorney.

"We'd be happy to accommodate your needs. I'll put you thorough to Rick Midori, who specializes in silver. And your name?" Felton asked.

"Jack Ripton." Shamus stifled a giggle. Greedy weasel wouldn't dodge a call from the Ripper, would he?

"One moment."

"Rick Midori speaking. How may I be of service?"

"Rick, hi. Shamus Ryan from Patriot Motors, how are you today?" Oh, if he could only see the confusion on that snotty face.

"Uh, I'm quite well. I was led to believe you were someone else."

"Just kidding around. Anyway, are we still on for seven o'clock tonight?" Shamus didn't care if Midori believed his dodge. He needed answers, dammit!

"As to that. Your call, despite the subterfuge, was propitious." He paused. "You know, propitious?"

It means "no sale," you arrogant, ass-wipe, dead man! "Go ahead."

"Regrettably, I won't be able to come in tonight. Can we reschedule for next week? How about next Monday, in the evening? You work evenings, I presume? I won't even darken the doorstep if you are not present. You have exclusive province over my business at Patriot."

"No problem, Rick. We'll see you on Monday. Why don't you leave a small deposit on the car so it won't get sold over the weekend?"

"No, no. I prefer to remain subject to the whims of fate."

"Okay then. We'll see you on Monday." Shamus forced a smile. Lying piece of crap. Just to be sure, a "whim of fate" would check his house after work. He lived out in Greenville, in the carriage house of one of the large estates. Shamus felt his muscles clench tighter and tighter for the remainder of his shift.

* * *

"How'd you make out today?" Mark Dey tapped him on the shoulder. Shamus jumped and fumbled with the buttons of his sport jacket.

"Huh? I was thinking about something."

"I used to do that, but I found it just got in the way."

"Yeah, right. I should have stayed in bed; I couldn't sell anybody today." Shamus picked up his keys.

"It happens. I sold one guy today, another mini-deal. Big whoop, but at least it will cover my time. I hope we'll have some good traffic tomorrow," Mark said, and he walked with him to the door.

* * *

Shamus started his car and turned up Pennsylvania Avenue. The city lights slipped behind him, and the landscape grew darker, along with his mood.

He passed the entrance to his apartment complex and the shopping center where Midori worked. Soon, the streetlights gave way to rolling hills and large houses. Lawns became grounds, and the houses hid beyond vast driveways. Some owners would rent out the carriage houses to have another person keep an eye on their property.

Rick Midori had lucked into a sweet deal. Undoubtedly, he was well acquainted with the upper-crust set, given his line of work, and he took full advantage. Shamus turned into the long driveway. Even at night, he could see that the grounds were immaculate. The main house was dark, and he hoped the owners were away. The carriage house was tucked in among some large trees.

Shamus could see a light on, and he prepared to turn his car around quickly though he saw no sign anyone moved inside the cozy little house. He didn't even have to get close before he glimpsed the distinctive outline of the small car in the moonlight. Nothing else shared the aerodynamic shape of the Insight.

Somebody needed a house call.

CHAPTER 19

Reservation

Newark, Delaware

Nelson got into Chang's BMW. "You know I don't like surprises."

"This place has the best Mandarin food you've ever tasted."

Nelson tugged at his collar. "Couldn't you find a place where I don't have to dress up?"

Chang could see that the brand-new oxford shirt chafed him, but at least he looked presentable. His own suit fit like it was made for him, which it was.

Chang sped around slower cars. Horns blared and headlights flashed.

"You trying to get pulled over?"

Chang pointed to his wallet where he kept his shield. "It's my prerogative."

"Where are we going?"

"Shu's House of Mandarin Delight."

"That sounds familiar... Hey, isn't your mother's helper or whatever named Shu?"

"Now that you mention it..."

Nelson looked like a trapped animal. "No. Turn around. I'm not having dinner with your mother."

"I knew you'd say that. She wants to meet you." Chang wished he knew why.

"She's lived a long life without my company."

"At least you'll get a great meal out of it. Shu's old-school authentic."

"Why me?"

"She won't say. I shouldn't have told her we're working a case."

* * *

Chang parked in front of the house, and before they reached the door Shu opened it. He wore a traditional "folk suit" made of black silk with a Mandarin collar and frog buttons down the front. Shu bowed.

"Good evening, Master Paul. Welcome, Master Rogers." Nelson bowed back. Shu bowed again and so did Nelson. Chang pushed Nelson through the door.

Shu led them into the house. Chang smelled pungent sandalwood incense. He watched Nelson scan the rare jade figurines in a display case.

"Are those…" Nelson's eyes grew large.

"Han Dynasty, we think about 100 BC." Chang marveled at the way Nelson absorbed and retained information.

"This puts your collection to shame."

It did. Chang liked his own pieces, but they were leftovers compared to the treasures here. "My father never lost his eye for quality. I wish she'd keep them safer."

"Come, gentlemen." Shu gestured toward the double doors that led to the dining room.

Chang stepped into the room and smiled at his mother, who sat at the head of a long rosewood table. When she stood, he could see her long flowing silk dress. It was dark blue and decorated with pink plum blossoms. She wore a necklace with a white jade pendant of a dragon. Fitting, Tai Kai could mean "Dragon Queen." He may have had his father's face, but he got her temper.

"Thank you for coming to my home, Mr. Rogers. I am happy to meet you at last."

"Please call me Nelson."

"Okay. I older, so call me Mrs. Chang." She gestured and Shu disappeared. He returned with a tray of steaming soup bowls.

"Bird's nest soup," Shu said.

Nelson frowned.

"Eat. It not kill you," she said.

Nelson sampled the broth. "This is good."

"I told you. Shu almost worthless, but he can still cook." She slurped her soup.

Chang drained his bowl. Perfect balance of spices. Shu stood by, and Chang could see the glimpse of pride on his impassive features. The old man was long immune to his mother's barbs. Shu cleared the dishes.

"Peking duck next. Traditional, not American," Tai Kai said.

"That means Shu leaves the fat on the skin. It's the best part," Chang said. Shu was an artist, and Chang wished he could taste his cooking more often.

"You have dinner with your mother," she prodded Nelson, "or do you make her eat alone like Paul?"

Nelson paused and looked at Tai Kai.

"I never knew my mother. I grew up in an orphanage and foster homes in New York."

"Foster?"

Chang explained in Mandarin. She nodded. Shu brought in the main course, and the three ate in silence. Chang savored the food and could just make out the strains of one of his mother's Chinese operas from hidden speakers. His "American" ears never appreciated the gongs, shrieks, and drones.

"Okay, you have excuse." She paused. "Why you want to become policeman?"

Nelson shrugged. "I always wanted to solve mysteries. It was the only thing I was good at."

"Paul tell you why he turn back on family?"

Here we go. "Mother…"

"You so proud. I tell him. After his Uncle Tuen killed, we want him to take over business. He know how, but he say no. Fight gang, make his father and mother leave. New York used to be civilized."

"Not everywhere," Nelson said.

"No. We leave jungle, he stay, grab tiger by tail."

"Not tigers. Rats," Chang said.

"Too many rats for one." Tai Kai pointed with her chopsticks at the scar on his neck.

"Or two." Nelson stared at the tablecloth. Tai Kai turned her gaze toward him.

"Paul say you work with him again."

"Just helping on a case. I'm not back with the police."

"You still crazy?"

Chang sprayed plum sauce. "Mother!"

Nelson exploded in laughter.

"They think they fixed me. I fooled them." Nelson looked at her. Tai Kai smiled.

"You got nice girl who take care of you?"

Nelson lowered his head. "Not anymore. She thought I was mysterious, but then she figured out I was just strange." He took a bite of duck.

In his mind Chang could see Carrie's bookworm face, and he felt anger swell up at the way she'd abandoned Nelson. He translated for his mother that Nelson met her at a library and they dated for a while, but it didn't work out.

At the time, Chang had found Nelson's late-night calls for advice tiresome. Back then he didn't understand how much Nelson lived in his own world and rarely showed romantic interest. Colleen had had no patience for Nelson and little with Chang's family.

When Chang was still with her, his mother would pronounce her name "Careen." Always bugged Colleen, but now Chang thought it summed up their relationship. "Careened" off the "criff."

"I know what you need. Shu!" Tai Kai spoke rapidly in Chinese. Shu's surprise broke through his façade.

"He does *not* need dried seahorse." Chang felt like an embarrassed kid again. Did it every time.

"Put yin in your yang!" Her sharp laugh reminded Chang of a seagull. "You watch out for Paul?"

"He takes care of himself," Nelson said.

"I not here forever. He need friend. Don't trust American girl."

"Mother, I'm not a piece of furniture. I'm sitting right here."

"I forget what you look like. I thought you were salesman with your European costume."

Chang stared at the ceiling. "You're going to outlive all of us."

"Western medicine going to kill me. You see."

"Mrs. Chang, have you ever thought about going back to China to visit?"

"China not a place. It here." She pointed to her head. "And here." She covered her heart. She paused. "Besides, too many Communists."

"I'll show your son how to keep women away." Nelson's voice was deadpan.

Her laugh filled the room. "You not crazy, you smart. Be careful. Too many bad people out there."

"Yes, ma'am."

Chang could see she had fun at his expense as usual but that the evening tired her out. After the meal, he and Nelson said goodbye.

Shu walked them to the door. Chang noted Shu didn't hand his partner a baggie from his stores of Chinese herbs and medicine. Nelson thanked him for the food.

Chang turned to leave but stopped when Shu and Nelson stared at each other. Neither appeared uncomfortable, and after what seemed to Chang like a long time, Shu gave a tiny nod.

"You live inside but give balance," Shu said to Nelson.

"Sorry?"

"You water, temper his fire." Shu indicated Chang.

Nelson looked at Shu like he was an exhibit. Shu tolerated the examination with his customary nonchalance.

"I can't read you." Nelson sounded amazed. "I get nothing but calm."

He leaned forward and inhaled deeply through his nose. "Wait…something…it's buried deep…intense…settled now." Nelson looked up. "You're good." He turned to Chang. "He's strong."

The corners of Shu's mouth hinted at a smile. "Thank you."

Details of Shu's past were still a mystery even after decades. The old man was more than a caregiver, but Chang respected his privacy. What did Nelson pick up?

CHAPTER 20
Soft Sell
Greenville, Saturday, last day of March

Whenever Saturdays fell on the last day of the month, the sales team would go nuts to push out cars. Shamus only had one delivery, and then he would be free to feast on the floor traffic.

Early in the day, his customer Myrtle Maynard came in with more questions about the Odyssey minivan. Some salesmen referred to the old lady as "Shamus's girlfriend." Shamus thought she might crack and put down a deposit today.

"I don't think I could put money down on anything without driving it first."

Of course not.

"I understand. It's such a popular vehicle. If I *could* get you a quick drive, would you make a decision?"

"I still don't want to rush into anything. But it would help." She smiled at Shamus.

"Have a seat. I need to do a little horse trading, but I might be able to work something out." He smiled back. Atta girl.

Shamus walked down to Dale's office, where his biggest cardinal rule was never to interrupt him when he was with customers. Few new salesmen who received his wrath repeated the mistake. Thankfully, his people weren't in yet.

"I'm gonna cut to the chase."

"That'd be nice." Dale didn't look up.

"I have a customer this close to putting money on an Odyssey." Shamus held his thumb and index finger an inch apart.

"No."

"Hang on, I know you're busy and you don't want anyone driving your van, but before you say no…"

"Already did." Dale continued with his paperwork.

"I'll buy you lunch. A good one. Some place Hank likes."

"Nope." Dale stopped working and looked at Shamus.

"Okay, lunch plus I'll throw in the new issue of *Playboy*."

"What makes you think I don't already have it?"

"Because you're cheap. I'll toss in five bucks worth of gas, too. My final offer." Shamus saw him weaken.

"Keys in my jacket pocket behind the door. You do most of the driving, and if there is so much as a scratch, it's coming out of your pocket." Dale returned to his work.

Jackpot! "You're the best!"

"Have fun and don't go parking."

Shamus retrieved the keys and returned to Myrtle.

"Great news! We can take our business manager's personal van out. It's the current model." He led her out the door.

After the drive, Shamus could feel her wanting to say yes, but her timid nature held her back. She loved the van.

"Shamus, thank you for everything you've done. I really appreciate it. But I'm a widow and my husband used to make these decisions. I have to sleep on it for a night or two.

I like the van, but it's a big decision for me. Thank you for not pressuring me."

Shamus almost said, "And thank you for not buying!"

"I understand. I'll give you a call next week to see how you're doing."

* * *

When he returned, another customer was waiting. She was young, maybe twenty. Caked-on makeup. A dirty girl, for sure. Wouldn't dare speak to her if he wasn't at work.

She had shoulder-length brown hair and wore a cropped T-shirt that exposed her tan midriff. A wispy tattooed face on her belly turned her pierced navel into a mouth that complemented the stud in her tongue. When she walked, the mouth opened and closed. Reminded Shamus of a blow-up sex doll.

Shamus felt a chill creep up his legs for even looking at her. Other salesmen stared and whispered. Act natural.

He introduced himself, and she said her name was Heather Cleary.

"I need a car." She had a raspy smoker's voice.

"Any particular model in mind?"

"You have any gold V6 Accord coupes?"

"We do. Are you familiar with the Accords?"

"I better be. I had one until two weeks ago. It got totaled, and I'm driving around this piece-of-shit rental. I *hate* it. I want my Honda back." She stomped her foot, and belly-face leered at him.

"I understand," Shamus said. It was an understanding kind of morning. "I'll bring the gold one around…"

"Don't you listen? I know how they drive, I just want it back. If you get some paperwork, I'm ready to take care of this today."

A quick sale. His kind of girl after all. "If we can get the car detailed, are you ready to take it today?"

"No. I have a massage scheduled in an hour. But if you give me a good deal, I'll sign today and give you a deposit or something."

He took her credit card to Jake, who got pissed off because she wouldn't take delivery until the following month.

"A what? If Little Miss Inky wants a great deal, show her this number and tell her it's only good until the end of today. Go close her!" Shamus saw he was three cars shy of his goal.

Heather looked at the number and asked, "Is that it?"

He started to explain and caught the bored look on her face. No attention span, but at least she seemed satisfied with the price.

"Okay, whatever, that's fine. Where do I sign, and what day can I pick up the car next week?"

Shamus tried to explain about the "today only" aspect of the deal.

"Oh, that is such bullshit! If you'll sell it today for that much, you'll do the same thing next week."

Shamus took a deep breath. Sex-doll called him a liar. Forgot what she's good for… Gonna lose her soon; spoiled slut isn't used to hearing the word "no."

"Okay, Heather. Sign here and give me your credit card for the deposit, and I'll clear it with the manager. Once I get his okay, we'll do a quick credit application and you're done." He handed her an application form and held out a pen.

She let Shamus keep his hand in the air while she dug into her designer bag and pulled out a gold Mont Blanc pen.

He closed his fist around the cheap plastic. Don't snap it. Shamus hustled back to Jake. He explained the situation. Jake shook his head.

"It's a shitty sale if it goes next week! I did that 'cause I need to hit my damn number." Jake looked over at her. "*I'll* give her a rubdown. Okay, a shitty sale is better than nothing." He signed off on the deal.

When she was gone, he felt better with a sale under his belt. Shamus thought about his evening plans and felt himself getting aroused.

CHAPTER 21

Blind Justice

The sun set, and Shamus lay sleepless on his bed. He couldn't rest, but his fatigue melted away when it was time to get started. Shamus grabbed his game bag and walked over to his dresser. He removed the snub-nosed revolver and opened the cylinder; a quick glance confirmed the weapon was loaded. Time to saddle up.

He recovered the car he'd picked out for the evening, a real junker traded in today. The drive took less than fifteen minutes. Shamus doused his headlights before the turn and slowed to a crawl up the driveway. The moon gave plenty of natural light, and he parked the car behind a thick stand of trees. He walked the remaining fifty yards with his bag over his shoulder.

Just one light burned in the second story of Midori's carriage house. The main house was completely dark. Very good. The Rickster probably watched the eleven o'clock news. Midori was about to *become* a current event. Shamus buried his face in the bag to muffle the whoop of laughter.

He hadn't gotten too close to the house last night and didn't know the layout of the front. Inspiration struck in the form of a tiny blinking red light coming from inside the new car.

Midori had bought an optional security system. Shamus crept closer and picked a good spot to hide near the front door. Midori had to be upstairs. He could hear the faint sounds of the television.

He tiptoed to the car, put one foot on the back bumper, and then jounced it with both his legs. The alarm pierced the night. The headlights flashed and the horn blared. Shamus dashed to his hiding place and waited for his quarry. He shrank back, and a shadow crossed the pool of light in the driveway. The alarm stopped. Shamus waited. Nothing else happened. The shadow retreated, and he could hear the television again.

Must have used the remote. The red light blinked when the alarm reset. Shamus ran and jumped on the front of the car. The alarm's sound and light carved into the tranquil night. Shamus saw the shadow reappear, but the racket continued for longer this time. Silent again.

He heard the click of the front door lock, and light splashed the front stoop. Shamus tried to become part of the wall just beyond the light and could see Rick in a bathrobe peering out at the dim driveway.

"Hello? Is someone out there? This isn't funny."

Shamus disagreed. Midori extended his arm out toward the car and cycled the alarm.

Shamus watched Midori step back and begin to close the door. Shamus pounced onto the door stoop and thrust his head into the gap. He brought his face within inches of Midori's and gave him both lungs.

"Booo!"

Midori leaped backwards and made a noise like he'd been punched in the gut. He fell on his butt, wide-eyed. His hands came up like feeble claws.

Shamus stepped inside and closed the door. He kept an eye on the twerp and held the gun at his side.

"Did I scare you? It's only me."

Midori didn't appear reassured. Shamus knew they were alone in the house. Midori wasn't married, and the single car outside meant no visitors. The fact that the guy was a jerk helped, too.

"Uh, uh, uh… Whuh, whuh." Midori stayed on the floor and sounded like an old car trying to start on a cold morning.

"Get it together, Rick. We have unfinished business. We can chat uninterrupted here. Now settle down; we can work this out."

Midori's gaze stayed glued to the gun. "You're thinking I was going to forget about you, didn't you? Sure you are. Said I'd take care of you, and that's exactly what I'm going to do. You helped me, and I'll help you. I'll get you the same commission. What's more fair than that?"

No vocabulary lesson. Good. "Take a breath and pay attention. I'm going to lay it out for you." Shamus looked into the main living room area. It was beautifully decorated and dominated by a comfortable couch with a matching chair that flanked a glass-topped coffee table.

"Sit still for a minute." Shamus crossed into the room and lowered the shades. He kept an eye on Midori.

"You'll have lots of questions, but please put this on first and don't say a word. Not even a big one." Shamus put his bag on the floor and reached in with his free hand. He took out a flat sleep mask. He tossed it to Midori.

"I'll explain everything, but I'd feel happier if you can't see. I can put away the gun. Unless you want me nervous and jumpy with a loaded pistol in my hand…"

Midori began to shake, but he managed to put on the mask. He would be blind while he wore it.

"Good job! Okay, on your knees, hands behind your back. Now we can talk without you running out and calling the police before we've reached an understanding. When we're done, I don't think you're going to want to turn me in." Shamus loved to soothe his toys. No wonder he was such a good salesman.

Midori allowed Shamus to duct-tape his arms behind his back and bind his legs. Shamus sat him up with his back against the couch and his legs extended in front of him.

"Comfy?" No answer. "It's okay to speak, but try to stay on topic. You tend to ramble."

"What do you want with me? I can give you money."

"Why does everybody always say that? Do I look like a thief? What I want is more precious than money. I need the truth. I'm a little concerned that might be the one thing you aren't willing to give me."

"I'll tell you anything."

"See, that's what I'm talking about. Don't tell me 'anything,' just the truth."

"I *meant* ask me anything."

"First of all, I'm leaving car sales and getting out of town, but I couldn't leave until I knew why you didn't buy from me. I need to know if you plan to send the cops after me."

"No! Just don't hurt me. I won't say anything, I promise."

"I want to believe you, but that car in your driveway… let's say it put the trust thing under a bit of a strain. I need a little more." Shamus felt himself shudder with anticipation. So much fun.

"What do you mean?"

"Really glad you asked. I've come up with a little game designed to...how might *you* put it? To promote integrity and decisiveness through the miracle of negative reinforcement." Shamus reached into his bag and pulled out a huge cigar.

"What?"

"Say, do you mind if I smoke?"

"No..." Midori sounded confused.

"You probably will."

CHAPTER 22
Brief Case

Chang wore his dress uniform, complete with blue tunic, pressed pants, and polished shoes. He heard Daisy's "recognition" bark. Nelson opened the door.

"You look uncomfortable," Nelson said, gathering his materials.

"It's tight. I don't wear it much anymore." Chang was glad the buttons were strong. He looked at Nelson's outfit, black trousers and an orange shirt with a deep-red tie.

"No good?" Nelson asked. Chang heard irritation in his voice.

"This is a briefing. You know the drill."

Nelson stomped upstairs.

Colonel Byrd balked at the prospect of civilian involvement, but Chang thought he made progress when he gave him an edited version of Nelson's background.

Unfortunately, Byrd's intention to run for governor next year made him hypersensitive to potential criticism in the press. Byrd was furious about the Flannigan article.

But Chang remembered that the obnoxious reporter at the *Daily Post* used to write for the *New York Times,* possibly when Colleen was there. After the divorce, Colleen had raced back to her old job in the city. She might have some inside dirt on Flannigan, or know someone who did. Wasn't a bad excuse to call her.

* * *

In the car, Chang mentally reviewed the case and what might convince Byrd he needed Nelson's insight.

Nelson broke the protracted silence. "You're worried."

"I hope Byrd goes with our idea, that's all."

"That's not all."

Just like a mind reader. "You'll do fine. It's only one person. We'll outnumber him."

"Can't be worse than poker night." Nelson chewed on a fingernail.

* * *

In the headquarters building, the two went to the outer office where "Colonel Byrd" was stenciled on the door. Chang removed his Smokey Bear hat, and they waited.

Patty, the civilian assistant, returned to her desk outside the office. "Can I get either of you anything? Coffee?"

"Yes, please." Nelson spoke instantly.

Chang cringed inside. Nelson never learned.

Patty picked up the phone. Chang could hear the buzz on the other side of the frosted glass door.

"Go right in. I'll bring your drink."

* * *

They walked into the office and took the two seats arranged in front of the desk.

"Detective, Mr. Rogers. Let's get started." Colonel Byrd stared at Chang from across his huge desk. He was a large man with a shaved head, wide nostrils, and bushy eyebrows. The first time Nelson saw a picture of Byrd, he told Chang it looked like two caterpillars crawling across a pink bowling ball. Sitting in Byrd's office, Chang said a quick prayer to his ancestors that today Nelson would keep the image to himself.

Pictures of Byrd with politicians and other police officers shared the wall with citations and awards. He seemed to know all the right people.

"Detective Chang gave me your background, but I'll say it's unconventional to involve a civilian, and I'm a conventional guy."

Byrd tapped his pen against his teeth. Chang couldn't remember if he was an ex-smoker or not.

"Rogers, if half of what the detective says is true, I'm impressed. 'Can't judge a book by its cover' comes to mind."

Byrd's pause grew into an uncomfortable silence that Chang finally took to mean he should begin.

He went over the murder timeline and their theory about a single killer.

"I've read the reports—different weapons, ethnicities, motives. What makes you think they're connected? And why does that weasel at the *Daily Post* seem to agree?" Byrd leaned back in his chair. Tap, tap, tap…

"I wondered myself, sir. I'll find out." Chang explained that they thought anger drove the killer and that the bizarre food uses were part of a ritual.

"Interesting, but I still don't see how you connect the dots to all three cases."

"I'll cover the physical evidence. Nelson will review behavioral impressions based on our years of experience. We have shoe prints from all three crime scenes. The tread patterns are different, but they're all the same size. No fingerprints, but we have similar hair and fiber from all three scenes. DNA should be back in another week or two.

"In the two cases where the victims were tied up, we found the same brand of duct tape. The one time he used handcuffs, they were the cheap kind that come from a magic or gag shop." Chang paused.

The door opened, and Patty came in with Nelson's coffee. Nelson yelped when he scorched his tongue. Byrd covered what Chang was sure was a smile.

When Chang described the bloody footprints at the Hubberts' and the overlooked valuables, Byrd seemed to take notice. He leaned forward and put his pen on the desk.

"But this doesn't explain what the victims have in common, why the guy is doing this, and the million-dollar question, what's next?" Byrd looked over at Nelson.

Nelson stood. He faced Byrd, but Chang was sure he really stared at the wall. "More killings."

"When?"

"Soon."

"That's it?

A drop of sweat crept down Nelson's temple. "We'll learn from each crime scene until we nail the guy."

Byrd's voice rose. "You always speak in riddles?"

Nelson looked crushed. Not the home run Chang hoped for.

"If you've never chased one of these guys, it can seem more random than it is." Nelson stopped when Byrd glared at him.

Careful. Byrd's ego was famous. So was his temper.

"I may not have worked my way up in New York City, but I didn't get this position by my looks." Byrd's voice dropped near a whisper.

No, thought Chang, your uncle was a state senator.

Nelson leaned over the table and took another sip of the coffee. "Ouch." He put the cup down.

"Colonel, here's my picture of the perp so far. Based on composite profiles of serial killers, this one's in his twenties, almost certainly white, has no significant relationships, especially romantic ones. Probably sexually dysfunctional and moderately successful in his job at best. His inadequacy drives him to express himself in ways that make him feel powerful." Nelson closed his eyes, and Chang saw Byrd frown, but he was riveted.

"He's venting a lifetime of rage at what he sees as symbols of his anger or perhaps the objects themselves. Don't yet know what he's angry about, but he'll get worse."

"How do you mean?" Byrd leaned toward Nelson, who opened his eyes.

"Look at the pattern. The first crime was a double, but he shot helpless victims in the head from behind. Whatever he was doing with the food was important to him. After his ritual, he killed them." Nelson paused. Byrd looked skeptical.

"Move up a week to the Patel murder. You know the facts. The killer took precious time to smash a lemon into the dead man's face. Why? He needed more violence. This time he looked his victim in the eye first. That's significant. Still, only two events. We weren't sure until the third crime scene."

Now Byrd was rapt.

"Last Monday. Again a double killing. Much more violent. The killer controlled his victims and enjoyed it. The autopsy shows that Mr. Hubbert had almost two bags of corn chips in his stomach. Mrs. Hubbert was suffocated. After she was dead, he jammed a loaf of French bread down her throat. Food again. Why? We still don't know, but a ritual plays through all three killings, only this time he forgot to stick to his plan. No theft."

"What do you mean?" Byrd began to chew his pen.

"It didn't go the way he expected, and he got mad. You see what he's capable of when he's angry." Nelson gestured to the grisly color photo of Doug Hubbert's crushed skull.

Chang reviewed the sequence of events and why they thought Doug put up a fight. Byrd listened, which gave Chang hope.

Nelson closed his eyes again. "He crossed a huge line, killed up close and personal. No shooting. He bashed a man's brains in, got splashed with blood and gray bits. Did he panic? No. He went upstairs, washed his hands in the master bathroom, walked to the closet, and we think stole a shirt. He would have brought his own if he planned on wet work.

"You might leave at this point… Does he? No. The luminol shows he went *back* to the basement and stopped on the stairs. Couldn't resist a final peek. That, Colonel, is what scares me the most." Nelson opened his eyes.

"You both think he's going to get more violent?"

Chang stood. "He likes the power. When he's in control, I wouldn't put anything past him. He did a quick kill on Mr. Patel, who you'll notice wasn't helpless. When he killed the Hubberts, he had time to play out his fantasies through his ritual. He is one of these guys who gets hooked on the rush, maybe even gets off on it. He's going to need more and more to do the job. Killers evolve and refine their technique, which might explain some of the differences in weapons."

Byrd wiped his forehead with his sleeve. "Anything else?"

Chang wished he could see Byrd through Nelson's eyes. "We still don't know how he chooses his victims, but it isn't random. I don't think it's racially motivated. He doesn't display any of the skinhead-type trademarks, he leaves no telltale graffiti, and his last victims were white." Chang knew that in Delaware it was almost impossible to find three groups of people with no connections whatsoever.

Byrd looked hard at Chang. Several seconds ticked off the wall clock before he spoke. "*If* I agree to let you pursue this, what's next?"

"With your permission, Nelson would work as a consultant and help me pull out the details that will break the case." Chang felt a spark of hope.

"Won't we break it without a civilian?"

"Colonel, if I may." Nelson interrupted. "This killer is going to keep it up until he's caught."

"And?" Byrd sounded impatient.

Chang said what he knew Nelson wouldn't. "Without Nelson's help, it will take longer. More people will die."

"I'll think it over and let you know. Until then, Detective, work this case yourself and through the proper channels, understand?"

"Yes, sir. I understand." But that didn't mean he agreed to comply. Sometimes Asian nuance could be useful.

CHAPTER 23

Call Back

Chang's house, Sunday night

Chang wiped his sweaty hands and picked up the receiver again. He dialed, paused. Deep breath. His finger stabbed down on the last number. It rang once. Twice. Maybe she's not home.

He heard the connection, and a sleepy voice made his heart hammer.

His mouth felt like cotton. Forgot the water. "It's me."

"Travis?"

The name felt like a punch in the gut. "Paul."

"Jeez. I'm sorry. You woke me up."

It was barely after eleven. Chang heard the flick of a lighter before Colleen inhaled. He pictured how sexy she looked when she did that.

"I can call another time."

"No. Got an early flight is all. You okay?"

"Not me. A case." Chang outlined the murders and the too-quick media appearance.

"Flannigan, huh? Cranky goblin?"

"What do you know about him?"

"Only met him once. He was drinking his way out of a job by then, but he's still a legend around here." She sounded awake now. He loved that honeyed voice except when she used it to yell at him.

"He's staging a comeback. I think he wants this case for a springboard."

Chang heard Colleen blow out smoke.

"You've got a pit bull on your hands, sweetie."

Chang knew it was a throwaway term, but it warmed him to hear her say that to him.

"If I were you, I'd work the leaker side. Flannigan wouldn't crack if you sicced your mom on him."

"There's a thought."

"How's she doing?"

Chang knew Colleen was only being polite. "She has good days and bad."

"Not sure what's worse." That husky laugh again. "And Shu?"

For an instant he thought she said, "And you?" but she'd already asked him. Tell her anyway. "Strong as ever. He's training me again. It's working better than any therapy would have. I feel like a new person. You'd be surprised." Stop babbling!

"That's great." Fake enthusiasm over ice.

He had gone too far. Chang punched himself in the leg and focused on the pain.

"Yeah. Want me to tell him Careen says herro?" Shu never minded her jokes.

"Sure. Hey, when I get back I'll ask around about Flannigan, okay?"

"I'd appreciate it." Chang resisted the urge to offer dinner.

"Well, nice catching up and all, but I gotta get my beauty sleep. Give me a buzz next time you're in the city." Chang said he would. He figured she knew he was lying. He didn't need a face to go with a name like *Travis.*

Sleep was out of the question. Chang spent the remainder of the night with the facts of the cases. His search through his notes for a common thread only yielded a headache. He skipped the aspirin and went straight for the jar of Shu's version of Tiger Balm. "Work better but smell like yak in heat." Shu didn't exaggerate, but it banished the pain in Chang's temples.

Chang meditated, drank ginseng tea, and stared at the crime scene photos. His imaginary canoe leaked, the tea left a bitter taste, and the photos swam in front of his eyes, but he pushed his ex-wife out of his mind for a few hours.

He was never lonely in the dark. The innocent dead filed in to accuse him. The Tongs' sister. Her face would drift among the masks. He tried and failed to forget her name… Tao, means long life. The gods laughed at him.

Most of all he could count on Jennifer Topper for an almost regular nocturnal visit. The real estate mogul's daughter was never far from his mind.

Maybe it was those damn missing-person posters. David Topper must have plastered half of Manhattan with them. Killer had to see them. Right under her name and photo, in big letters: "GREEN EYES." Like that was unique. They were in the end, weren't they? Chang could still see those disposable wraparound sunglasses on Jennifer's face. The forensics guys called them geezer shades. They looked out of place on the smooth-skinned young girl. She could have been a passed-out party gal in her tennis whites, stoned and asleep on the tennis court that morning.

But she wasn't. He knew she was not some spoiled rich kid the day she invited him to speak to her class about investigations. Chang never forgot the lunch he ate with her in the school cafeteria afterward.

She'd told him about "Saving Face," the foundation she begged her father to create and fund. She became personally involved and helped arrange flights and corrective surgeries for Chinese children born with facial deformities. She told Chang that she saw them during a tour of China when she was fourteen and couldn't forget them. Jennifer said that after that experience was when she knew charity balls and fundraisers weren't going to be enough. She needed to help on a more personal level.

Jennifer was the kind of person who made a difference. Half the people Chang saved didn't seem worthy of the effort. David Topper cancelled funding a month after she was killed. "Couldn't bear the memories," he'd said.

Chang remembered the dew in her hair. After they removed the glasses, he saw the fuzzy green tennis ball pieces in place of her eyes. That's what stuck in his mind.

Enough. Chang wrenched his mind back to the case and jotted down some of the most fundamental things the three victim sets had in common. Had he missed something obvious?

Food, was that the common link? Did they share a favorite restaurant? The Nguyens and Mr. Patel sold food and didn't strike Chang as the types who would have eaten out very often. Certainly the Hubberts were interested in food.

All the victims lived in Delaware and were killed late at night. Why? Did they reside near where the killer lived or worked? The ages of the victims ranged between their thirties and forties.

They all owned their homes. So? They bought things and sold things in some capacity. Something about that twitched his radar, but what? Everyone buys things. Some sell, others just throw things away or donate them. Everyone buys things… He jumped when the phone rang. It wasn't Colleen.

CHAPTER 24

In the Bag

Monday morning

"One of these days you're going to get tired of being right." Chang relayed to Nelson over the phone what the duty officer just told him. Another victim.

"Where?"

"It's on an estate in Greenville, out Route 52 near the state line. I'm on my way now. Meet me up there. You'll see my unit at the entrance. I'll wait."

"You got the okay from Byrd?"

"He hasn't said no." Not yet.

"I'm to stay away until he makes a decision."

"That was before we got a new case." No time to argue.

"He needs control, maybe more than you. It's written all over him. We don't want to make him mad."

Chang squeezed down on the cell. He eased off before he crushed it. "That's my problem. Are you coming or not?"

"Half an hour."

Chang knew Confucius never said, "It is easier to ask for forgiveness than permission," but he thought the sage would approve anyway.

* * *

Chang met Nelson at the entrance to the estate. The iron gates opened to a long driveway. Along the way he could see a small carriage house and atop the hill a huge stone mansion with tall chimneys at both ends. Fingers of ivy climbed up one side.

"You made good time." Chang watched Nelson duck under the yellow tape.

Nelson's head swiveled during the walk up the driveway. Halfway to the carriage house two evidence techs unpacked their kits from the crime scene investigation van. Chang led Nelson over to meet them.

Chang introduced William Logan and Theodore Bristol. "Nelson's an experienced profiler. Treat him as an authorized consultant."

"Just call us Bill and Ted. Everyone else does," Bill said.

"Whether we like it or not." Ted flashed a friendly grin. His hair looked like a Brillo pad.

"Spotted something on my way in." Nelson pointed toward a stand of trees off the driveway about fifty yards from the carriage house. "Look between the trees and the driveway. You'll see tire tracks in the soft dirt. Killer must have parked there and snuck up to the house on foot. Try to get some footprints, at least the size."

Bill and Ted looked to Chang. "Go ahead. My say so," Chang said. Everyone lived in a CYA world.

"We'll start with photos. If there's an impression big enough, we'll go for a plaster cast." Ted picked up an evidence kit.

"I want to know if footprints lead up to the house and not straight up the driveway like a normal person would walk. Do we have a clear fix on time of death?" Chang itched to get inside.

"No later than Saturday night," Bill said and joined Ted. They moved toward the tracks.

Chang turned to Nelson. "We got word this morning from the victim's boss. He decided to check on the victim after he didn't come in or call. He said that was very out of character. The door was unlocked, and he saw the body."

Nelson took out a handkerchief and blew his nose. He leaned over the doorknob and sniffed. "Lotion. Did the witness touch the victim or walk around the place?"

"No, our guys told me he took one look and backed out. He's over at Troop One to give a statement."

"I'm more interested in what the victim has to say." Nelson reached for his crime scene outfit.

Chang handed Nelson the suit, gloves, and booties. He put on his own.

"Hang on a second." Nelson stopped Chang on the doorstep, looking on both sides of the stoop. Nelson spoke softly toward the floor. "There you are."

Chang hung back and watched his partner, a bloodhound on the trail.

Nelson pointed out distinct footprints in the soil on the right side of the front stoop. "You waited here, didn't you?" Nelson looked at the door. "Got him to open it, too, unless you're a locksmith."

No scratches around the lock. A faint trail led through the dirt and to the gravel of the driveway. The indents led over to the Honda parked in the driveway. The alarm light still blinked its warning even though the owner would never drive it again.

Chang walked over to the car and made sure he didn't touch it or spoil the indents that encircled half the vehicle. He spotted a shoe mark on the front bumper and on the back. He called Nelson over and showed him.

"Kicked the guy's new car, did you? Why?" Nelson looked again. "No, you didn't kick it, you jumped on it. Got both feet involved back here, looks like. Why?"

Chang noticed the blinking red light again. "Very clever. I think I know how he got this guy to open the door. Do you see how the dents in the gravel are deeper leading away from the marks on the bumper?"

"Oh, yeah."

"The killer jumped on the bumper and ran over there." Chang pointed to the spot beside the stoop. "His tracks are all over, but not on the other side. He ran. The added force made deeper divots. He wanted to hide after he set off the alarm. See the light?"

"That's pretty good. So, the victim opens the door and in pops our guy, but why the marks on the front and the back?"

"Maybe the killer had to do it a couple times before he would come out. Some of them will false-alarm even when a loud motorcycle goes by, which is why nobody pays attention to them most of the time." Chang knew Nelson wasn't up on the latest technology.

Nelson shrugged. "Could be. Ready to talk to the dead?"

CHAPTER 25

Fame and Fortune

Shamus's apartment, early Monday morning

"Okay, Gran. Once more then back to the cooler. I have to get ready for work." Shamus brushed tears of laughter out of his eyes. He picked up the folded copy of the early edition of the *Daily Post.* He'd have to buy another. This Flannigan turned out better than he'd dared hope.

He took a napkin, wiped the condensation off the urn, and straightened Gran's picture. He could swear there was a trace of a smile on her face. Why not? He picked up the paper and read aloud.

The Iceman Cometh
By Patrick Flannigan

This column has waited for a more forthcoming attitude from Delaware's thin blue line, but the state police continue to hoard their candor. The public has suffered as a result. We are compelled to reveal what they will not. Wilmington has a serial killer in its midst.

We can now confide to our readers that our source appears to be the killer himself. For reasons of his own, he contacted us to shed light on his motivation. He reaches us anonymously, so we do not know his identity, but we have corroborated his information and believe he is who he claims to be.

He calls himself "The Iceman." His message is as cryptic as it is simple. "Takers beware. They know who they are." We don't wish to speculate on the meaning of the warning, but we do want to ask a larger question.

Why do the police continue the charade that our city suffers only from a statistical blip of unconnected homicides? The lead investigator, Paul Chang, refuses to discuss the issue. A background investigation uncovered that this "wily veteran" left the NYPD in disgrace following the death of real estate mogul David Topper's daughter, Jennifer. Her body was found dumped on a public tennis court.

Is this really the best that they can do?

Inside sources with the state police indicate they have begun to shift additional resources to assist with the case, but the public face of the investigation would have us simply go about business as usual.

When we know more we'll pass it along. In the meantime… Tennis, anyone?

"Gotta go, Gran." The fear this column would spread got him excited, and he wanted her tucked away before it became obvious. He hoped Chang liked the write-up, though he might be a little busy. Someone must have noticed Midori was missing by now.

CHAPTER 26

Ashes to Ashes

Greenville

The small carriage house mimicked the design of the mansion. The neatly furnished interior showed restrained good taste, but Chang saw first-rate pieces wherever he looked. The living room sat just inside the foyer, to his left. Chang smelled stale cigar smoke. The lowered blinds created a dim atmosphere, but he saw the body immediately.

Midori was slumped over sideways from a sitting position with his back against the couch. Chang couldn't see the face clearly due to the plastic bag, but the telltale silvery tape shone in the dim light. The hair on Chang's neck rose. He envisioned the killer gazing down on his work.

They moved into the room, and Chang saw now that the victim wore some sort of mask over his eyes. A blindfold?

Midori's bathrobe hung open and showed boxer shorts and numerous quarter-sized burn marks up and down his legs and chest.

When Nelson spoke, Chang could hear the excitement in his voice. "Those wounds still hum with pain. Smell the smoke? Killer's got a taste for torture."

Chang concentrated and tried to see through the Dragon's eyes. Should be safe. Eyes only, what do you see?

His senses opened to absorb detail down to the stink of burned flesh and emptied bowels. When he got home, he would take a long shower to get the sensations off his body. Right now he needed to feel.

In the foyer Chang squatted to look for footprints, but he didn't see any on the thin rug that covered the floor. He did notice a scuff near the entrance, marked by traces of dirt. He checked upstairs and saw no sign of disturbance, same as in the kitchen.

Chang returned to the living room. Nelson stood nearby and stared at the body.

"It doesn't look like he was in the kitchen or upstairs, but it's hard to tell because the rugs are so thin." Chang stepped near the body. The bag over Midori's head read "Sandy's Dry Cleaning" along with an address on Union Street in Wilmington. Below the logo and address in smaller print it said, "Warning: NOT a toy. Bag may cause suffocation."

Chang looked closer at the burns on the chest and legs. The killer used a huge cigar. He'd seen enough cigarette burns from domestic cases, and the ashes in the burns left little doubt. Up close, Chang could tell from the discolored circular areas that the killer had burned the face as well. He left the bag for the evidence techs to remove.

Though the rug was too thin for footprints, he saw a couple cylinder-shaped piles of ashes that would help identify the type of cigar. He flagged them.

Nelson gestured toward the body. "Did his work right here. Less messy than Hubbert, but this guy suffered. Tied up with the same kind of tape. Blindfolded this time."

"It's worse than the Hubberts. He went berserk with the hammer, but at least it was quick." Chang felt anger begin to simmer under the horror. "This guy died hard; the perp took his time." He yanked on the reins and blinked away the Dragonsight.

"Yeah. He's gone into rigor, backs the tech's timeframe." Nelson got a blank look. He began to rock, and his rhythmic hum now came out as an unintelligible mumble.

Chang tried to put himself in the killer's skin. He knew Nelson could. Shower's not going to be enough. Deep meditation later, a thorough cleansing.

Nelson broke his trance and frowned at the body. "You're sure the kitchen showed no signs of disturbance?"

"Not that I could tell. We'll know more when we dust it. Why?"

"What's missing here?"

Chang felt a jolt in his brain. "No food or food-related action. No bread, chips, or lemons. Where's the signature?"

"Exactly. Unless they find a can of soup shoved up his ass or something, this is different." Nelson's eyes glittered.

Chang peered at the plastic. "Maybe the bag is the signature this time. We might be on the wrong track with food. What if it just happened to be food three times in a row?" He traced a gloved finger under the text printed on the bag. "Do you see what this says? That's his idea of a joke. After he was done torturing him, this was the killer's punch line." Chang walked to the foyer.

Nelson shuffled after him. "It's the rituals. They're all jokes. The Hubberts were overweight, and he stuffed bread in Maisy and made Doug eat a huge amount of Doritos. With Patel... What's funny about a lemon? You make a face because it is sour? Why the cans of food with the Nguyens?" Nelson closed his eyes.

"He thought it was funny." Chang could feel traction. "Keep going." Chang's radio squawked, and the tech team asked if they could get started inside. He told them to come in.

Bill and Ted swooped in and began to collect evidence. They told Chang about the tire tracks and that they'd spotted a couple of footprints in the dirt by the base of the trees. It hadn't rained since Friday, and the techs had poured several plaster casts.

Chang joined Nelson to look at the car again. Strange little thing. Chang knew about the new wave of eco-friendly cars that used part gas engines and part electric. He explained to Nelson, who wasn't a car guy, about hybrids.

Eco-friendly… Was Midori an environmentalist? He didn't remember anything about the Hubberts that made him think environmentalists. What about the Nguyens and Mr. Patel?

Ted stuck his scruffy head out the front door to let him know they were ready to remove the bag.

Bill got to the point. "What a sick son of a bitch."

"Ted, can you lift up that mask for me?" Chang willed himself not to see tennis balls.

"Sure." Ted slid up the mask. Despite horrible burns on the upper face, the area under the mask was untouched. Glassy eyes stared back. Brown.

Chang imagined the victim's anguish sitting there blindfolded, not knowing when the next hit would come. "He had the mask on the whole time, didn't he?" Chang forced the anger to stay down. Fogged his mind when it took over.

"Increased the killer's control. Can't run if you're blind, right? Tough to fight if you're helpless. He's cruel, but he's a coward." Nelson turned toward Bill and Ted. "Did the perp go upstairs?"

"We don't think so. All the prints we lifted seem to match the victim." Bill began to pack up the evidence and his case.

Nelson still wore his suit and gloves. "Going to check something. Be right back." Nelson climbed the staircase.

The techs left Chang alone with the body. He heard a whoop and "Yes!" shouted down the stairs. Nelson appeared moments later and held a fistful of plastic bags in his gloved hand.

Nelson came down the stairs and showed Chang. "Do you see?"

"What?"

"Look! Dry cleaner bags. *Midori's* dry cleaner bags! I found them in his trash. Check out the name on them." Nelson spread one out and held it up for Chang to read.

"'Greenville Dry Cleaning: Since 1978.' What's so... Hey!"

"They all say that. Of course he would use the place closest to his work. The killer *brought* the other one. He didn't get inspired. He brought the Sandy's bag on purpose."

Impressive. "Maybe he got lazy and grabbed what he had around his own house. Sandy's is a big dry cleaner over on Union Street, but this could be a little break."

"There are no little breaks, only little investigators." Nelson sounded giddy.

CHAPTER 27

Laughs Last

Patriot Motors, Friday afternoon

Shamus's good mood evaporated. Almost five o'clock and no sign of his delivery. Four hours late for this dirty little brat from last Saturday. He put in a bunch of calls to her house. She lived with her parents but must have her own line or cell phone. All he got was her voice mail.

Now it looked like it might rain. Just perfect. He would have to put the cleaned and detailed car back out on the lot because Hank had a delivery at five. Damn. He was certain he'd been stood up, but she'd have to contact him at some point. Patriot had her five-hundred-dollar deposit.

The dealership enjoyed a good day, but he remained stuck on the sidelines. He paced the floor and waited for this princess to show up or cancel. He watched Tommy and Mark snag some juicy retiree sales.

He fought boredom by thinking about the explosion of media coverage after the discovery of Midori and the wonderful Flannigan piece. The other news outlets finally caught on that an artist was at work. They stuck to hackneyed terminology in their headlines like "Serial Killer?" or "Psychopath on the Loose: Police Stumped by Mysterious

String of Homicides," but he supposed they didn't know any better. If they wanted the truth, a visit to "The Blarney Stone" would do the trick.

He saw from the articles that the police were holding back some details, but he could tell they were baffled. He culled Takers who wouldn't be missed from the herd. Besides, he'd been careful. Not all the cops were stupid.

What would they find? He wore gloves, changed his shoes and his cars. Even if he overlooked something and the cops managed to lift a fingerprint, he didn't have a record. Came close to arrest in Ohio when he went through a little fire-setting phase as a kid, but he'd stuck mostly to trash cans so there hadn't been too much fuss.

Shamus shivered. Just the thought that thousands of people all over Delaware worried what he "might do next" gave him goose bumps.

He covered his corkboard wall at home with newspaper articles full of nonsense about what might drive someone to "torment his victims" and what the cigar might signify. Rubbish. Midori was lying scum who only got burned when he refused to be honest. He was a better person by the time Shamus had finished with him.

Now the sweetness of those moments soured, all because of one filthy, pierced little slut. He shouldn't let it get to him. All part of the game, but he played by new rules.

Shamus sneered at the sound of thunder. Rain started to fall, and Jake yelled at him to move the car so Hank could get his under cover. Shamus climbed behind the wheel of the shiny coupe. Even the scent of leather mingled with the famous new-car smell failed to lift his spirits. He lingered inside the car and watched the water bead up and roll off the freshly waxed hood.

Back inside, Shamus saw that the only thing that was dried up was the flow of customers. The rain ran down the large showroom windows like a giant windshield. He looked away when his phone rang.

He answered, but there was nothing on the other end.

"Hello?"

"You must be sooo pissed." A sleepy voice finally responded. Shamus recognized Heather Cleary, and for a moment he thought maybe it had been a misunderstanding after all. Probably got another tattoo.

"Heather, is that you? Did you want to reschedule the delivery?"

"Not exactly." She giggled, and Shamus realized she wasn't sleepy, she was stoned. "I need my deposit back."

"Why?"

"Because I got my Beamer in the garage already. My golden German." She giggled again.

"You bought a different car? I thought you decided on another Honda." Shamus wanted to pound his head against the wall. No, make that *her* head.

"That's what the other Honda guy said when I just called him to get my other money back. You aren't allowed to yell at me like he did. He was an asshole."

"You put money on two other cars?"

"No. I...put...money on...threeeeee other cars!" She laughed out loud.

"Three other cars. Why?" His head started to buzz.

"I went to you, then I went to Marlo and they gave me a better price, and then I went to Lexus. I loved it, too. Then I went and saw the BMW. You know what?"

"What?"

"The Beamer is the Lexus of German cars, so I got it!"

Shamus almost hung up on her when she wouldn't stop laughing.

"So," she said, still giggling, "when can I get my money back?"

"Well, Heather, normally it can take up to ten days to clear the office—"

"Ten days, bullshit! I want it back now or my dad will sue your ass off. He's a hot-shit lawyer. I don't remember, what kind of ass did you have, anyway?" More laughter.

Something tore in Shamus's head. He should move on; after all, she charged money to his dealership. Five hundred bucks.

The wind picked up outside, and Shamus could swear he heard that cowbell Gran rang to call him in for punishment. He saw her face outlined in the raindrops on the showroom window. The sounds of the dealership grew faint.

He imagined wet sawdust tickling his legs, and he shivered with cold. No! This girl can be connected to me. Her deposit left a paper trail.

He could smell the icehouse and almost expected to see his frosty breath. Shamus pulled at the back of his pants. Gran found a new way to scream at him. I *can't.*

His crotch went numb. Maybe it was possible...

His chair now felt dry. The face melted off the window, and he could smell the Armor All on the showroom tires again.

"You still there, ass man?"

He tried to sound polite. "No need to get your dad involved. Tell you what. I'll bring the money by your house first thing Monday morning. I'll get cash and bring it myself.

Quicker than a check in the mail." He looked to see if any other salesman had heard the conversation. None had.

"Whatever, just give me my money!"

"First thing Monday, and please think of Patriot if you ever want another Honda."

"And please think of my dad if you ever want a new ass!"

Shamus hung up.

After Hank completed his delivery, the showroom emptied of customers. Always eager to fill the void, he came out of his cubicle with a fancy shopping bag for show and tell.

Shamus tuned him out. The rain continued unabated.

CHAPTER 28

Slip of the Tongue

Monday morning

Shamus never wanted a weekend to come and go as much as this last one. On Saturday it rained, and he started the day with yet another call from Myrtle. She told him she didn't want to negotiate in the rain. Did she think he'd make her stand in the middle of the parking lot? By the afternoon, he'd sold two cars, including a spot delivery to customers who were downright pleasant. Good to keep busy. "Idle hands are the devil's plaything," was one of Gran's favorites.

Sunday he barely managed to drag himself out of bed, but the whole day turned around at the bagel shop. He sat with his coffee and was reading the paper when he overheard two guys in the booth behind him start to talk about the killings. "Why can't the cops catch this guy?" "What else aren't they telling us?" "Scary. Who's next?"

Shamus congratulated himself on not turning around. He heard the fear in their voices and something else. Respect? Could be. Part of him wanted to offer his autograph. He was a star!

No way he'd answer their question about who was next. Too bad, he couldn't even tip off Flannigan. This one was going to be his little secret. Heather was too close, so Gran would just have to accept the compromise. Shamus spent the remainder of Sunday working on a disguise.

Mondays he wasn't due in to work until the early afternoon, so he had time, and he wanted to make sure Heather was alone when he dropped by to bring her what she needed. He packed everything up and stuffed some change into his pocket. He wore painter's coveralls over his work clothes and donned a painter's cap and sunglasses. A pair of cheap sneakers he'd never wear again completed his outfit.

By nine thirty he'd driven through the gorgeous winding back roads from Greenville to North Wilmington. Heather's folks had a nice place not too far from the Hubberts', though in a much fancier development called Garden Ridge. He passed the house and pulled into a nearby gas station. He dropped a pair of quarters into a pay phone.

After four rings Shamus felt irritation when the call rolled over to Heather's voice mail. He knew she was home. He hung up without leaving a message and realized the money was gone since the call went through.

He used his last coins to call again. This time he let it ring three times before he redialed. He repeated this procedure until she picked up.

"This better be good." He heard the drowsiness in her voice.

"Good morning!" he boomed into the receiver and then settled his voice so commuters wouldn't hear his name. "It's Shamus from Patriot. I have your deposit, Heather."

"My what?"

Shamus pictured the gears in her head grinding.

"Your deposit."

"Oh, yeah. You can send me a check. It's okay."

"I'm just around the corner. I have cash, but if you want a check instead…"

"Cash? Okay. Can you be here soon? Or why don't you slide it under the door?"

"Five minutes, but I must hand it to you personally and get a receipt. Otherwise they'll never reimburse me." He knew she'd jump on the cash.

"Just hurry up. My parents are at work, and I was sleeping."

"You'll be out cold before you know it. See you soon." Shamus wiped off the phone and hung up.

CHAPTER 29

Full Disclosure

Monday morning

Chang detested politics almost as much as administrative interference. Today he and Nelson would confront a perfect storm.

Media pressure meant intense political heat. The governor's office and a representative from the attorney general wanted a briefing on the case, and the colonel "suggested" that Chang bring Nelson. Nelson speculated that it was a good sign, but Chang knew better. The colonel was up to something. Maybe he could make some allies in the meeting.

Nelson said little in the car. Chang broke the silence. "There will be a few more people in the meeting, but nothing you can't handle."

"I hate this crap." Nelson could get cranky when he was nervous. "Any luck on the dry cleaner bag?"

"There were some smudges, but nothing we could use. I'm more optimistic about the hair samples. At least that could tie the same person to all the crimes."

"We already know that."

"We'll add it to our profile and pull Sandy's customer records. Maybe we can get a composite sketch that someone will recognize." Make it sound plausible to the politicians.

"Long shot."

"It's the most proactive thing I can think of until we nail the link between the victims."

"It's right there, I can feel it." Nelson ran his fingers through his hair.

"Is your scalp itchy yet?" Chang knew it would tingle when Nelson was close to a flash of insight.

"A little."

* * *

Chang and Nelson stepped into the conference room near Colonel Byrd's office. Chang felt everyone's eyes turn toward them. He resisted the urge to ball his fists, but he could smell a fight.

Byrd was already seated at a large circular table. Two civilian representatives sat next to him. Chang was surprised to see a friendly face. Nancy Brand, from Governor Spiker's office. Her smile reminded him of Colleen's, like she knew something he didn't.

Nancy was in her early thirties and a knockout. Tall, great figure, sharp. Too bad she pulled her hair back in such a severe style. He'd met Nancy when he joined the force. The governor was eager to showcase her diversity program, and Chang felt like the latest toy. Nancy was sent to parade him around. She seemed embarrassed by the spectacle.

Chang remembered her kindness and the spark of attraction he'd smothered. He was still with Colleen during what he now realized marked the beginning of the end of their marriage. He hadn't seen Nancy since the divorce.

Nick Fargo, from the attorney general's office, was a young guy with a smug mouth and predatory eyes. Chang disliked him on the spot.

"Come in, gentlemen." Byrd made the introductions and jumped right in. "What new information or leads do you have? Keep in mind we've read your initial reports."

Chang saw Fargo appraise Nelson and lean over to whisper something to Byrd. Both laughed, and Byrd mouthed "could be." Political weasels.

He glanced at Nelson. Uh oh. Nelson had "sponge face." He was absorbing every facial cue from the people around the table. He would know their frame of mind and might take it to heart. No time to talk him down now.

"Yes, sir," Chang jumped in. "I'll start with what we've learned and how it fits into what we already know and then let Mr. Rogers fill in the gaps." Chang felt like a player in Japanese Kabuki, just going through the motions toward a predetermined end.

He described how they thought the killer wore gloves and switched shoes, given the footprints and lack of fingerprints.

Fargo shook his head. "That's not good enough in court, officer."

Chang gripped a pencil and pictured a snowy field.

"We're still in the early stages of our investigation. Right now we're trying to develop a picture of the killer and a link between victims." A white blanket to cover the shrubs and grass…

"Please go on." Byrd appeared to be enjoying himself. Had he waxed his head? Or did it always look that shiny?

Chang presented the information on the dry cleaner bag at Midori's. "We think the killer may have made an oversight while trying to make a statement."

Nancy looked up from her notes. "Statement?" A strand of her hair escaped the bun, and she wound it around her finger. Chang broke off his gaze and cued Nelson.

Nelson stood and opened his mouth. Nothing. He closed it and swallowed. Chang heard a dry click. Nelson took a sip of water and spilled some on his papers. The silence filled the room. Chang tried to project calm to give Nelson something positive to read. Fargo whispered again, and Byrd looked like he struggled not to laugh. Only Nancy looked receptive.

If Nelson could just break the ice, say anything, then he'd be able to give his presentation.

"Just tell them what's on your mind, partner."

Byrd and Fargo snorted.

Nelson found his voice. "We're not."

Byrd's laugh settled into a thin smile. "Sorry?"

"We're not gay."

Byrd sputtered and turned very pink. "What?"

"Nope. Just sensitive. Get that a lot, though." Nelson jerked his thumb toward Chang. "He used to be married, and I almost had a girlfriend once." Was that a proud smile?

Chang felt the burn sear from his neck up to his ears.

"Yes, well…I had in mind a less freewheeling discussion, Mr. Rogers." Byrd regained his composure. Nancy flushed red and stared at her notes.

"Me too, but it's distracting to try talking past your phobia."

"I don't..."

Nelson raised his hands palms out. "I'm not judging. Just glad to correct the record. May I proceed?"

Byrd looked like he'd just tasted something bitter. "Please do."

Nelson recapped the rituals and put forward their theory that the signatures were jokes, not food. "We think the killer was so focused on displaying the warning that he forgot that the name and address of the source are printed on the bag."

"The killer may use this dry cleaner," Chang said. "Unfortunately, thousands do." He was relieved to have the conversation back to business.

Byrd scowled. "What if he does? What are we supposed to do, arrest every customer?"

"Sir, it would be premature to stake out the dry cleaner, but we know more about what he looks like than you might think." Chang could hear the wind begin to howl on his imaginary snowy field.

Nelson smacked his lips. Nervous, dry mouth, but he managed to speak. "Detective Chang is correct. We've isolated that the killer has reddish-brown hair, Caucasian-type."

"So far, so good. But how do we use that with the dry cleaner?" Tap, tap, tap went Byrd's pen against his capped front teeth.

"We want to interview employees and ask them if they have a regular customer who fits the description. We could narrow down a list from the customer base." Out of the corner of his eye, Chang saw Fargo shake his head.

Fargo leaned toward Chang. "Wait a second. I deal in facts. We don't know for sure the killer uses this dry cleaner. He could have pulled the bag out of the trash, for all we know. It seems like a big waste of time chasing shadows when we should concentrate on if these crimes really are all connected."

This kid had never investigated a homicide. Fargo was just close enough for a hard punch. A blizzard buried Chang's snowy field, and he broke the pencil with a loud snap.

Nelson jumped at the sound but spoke up, and Chang used the moment to collect himself. Byrd's smirk didn't help.

"Yes, sir, you raise an excellent point. We try our best to deal with the facts, but you probably know that we also have to operate on instincts." Nelson's voice cracked, but he hung tough.

"I can't be expected to build a prosecution against ghosts and hunches," Fargo said. "I need hard evidence, or this killer will just walk out the door." Fargo glowered at Chang and ignored Nelson.

"Once we have a suspect, I think we'll see things resolve quickly, Mr. Fargo. You'll have everything you need *when* it's your turn to get involved directly." Chang kept his voice level but locked eyes with Fargo. Fargo thanked him and stared back.

Chang continued. "On another front, we've all read the Flannigan columns. I'll speak to him, but I'm not optimistic. If what he says is true, can we obtain a warrant to monitor his phone or stake him out?" Give the worm a chance to be helpful.

Byrd used his best phony scold voice. "Chang, you know better than to even ask."

What Chang knew was that Byrd would throw Flannigan in the Brandywine River if he could get away with it. "Well, sir, it seems likely the killer will reach out to him again."

Fargo shared a look with Byrd. "You want to screw up our case before we can get near the guy?"

Ah, so. Birds of a political feather. Could he trust anyone in the room?

"If we can't catch him, your point is irrelevant. Whose side are you on?" Chang knew it was always whatever side helped Fargo.

Fargo turned to Byrd. "I don't have to take this."

He sounded like a petulant child.

Byrd held up a hand to call for silence. "We're all on the same side. Chang, see what you can find out on the dry cleaner. We might get lucky."

"Yes, sir."

"Another thing. Given the blistering criticism from our little friend at the *Daily Post,* you should leave him alone. Likewise, despite the apparent fact that Mr. Rogers is not preoccupied with a social life, for now he is not to be involved in the case in any way until we decide otherwise. No civilians. Is that clear?" Byrd looked at him hard, and Chang gave him an inscrutable wall.

"Of course, sir."

Nancy Brand raised her hand. "I have a dumb question."

Classic hands, like a sculpture. She could be stunning if she allowed herself to be.

"Yes?" Byrd said. Did Chang see a trace of annoyance?

If Nancy saw it she gave no indication. "With all the publicity, what are the chances the killer will lay low or get out of town?"

Nelson spoke up. "Anything is possible, Ms. Brand. But he won't."

Nancy looked at him. "How do you know that?"

"Loves the attention. Killings just about once a week. If anything, he's overdue. The whole city is afraid of him, and he's never felt so alive. Would you stop?"

Nancy shuddered. "Sorry I asked."

Chang felt an irrational urge to protect her. "Don't be. That's how we'll catch him. He's made mistakes. He'll make more."

"I wish that made me feel better." Nancy smiled again.

Chang wondered what she looked like with her hair down.

CHAPTER 30
No Signature Required

Chang slammed the car door. "You haven't lost your touch." He knew his sarcasm stung Nelson.

"What?"

Chang didn't answer.

"Oh, the first part? But it's true. Besides, you know I hate doing presentations. My mouth is still dry. Think it helped?"

"With who?" Chang blew out his breath. "Forget it. Byrd'll let me know." He had no business wanting Nancy Brand's phone number anyway. Chang pulled a bottle of water from under the seat and tossed it to Nelson.

Chang's cell phone rang. He picked up and listened for a moment.

"Another?" Nelson almost spilled his water when Chang mashed the accelerator.

"We'll see when we get there." Wiggins was calling from the scene, and Chang trusted the man's instincts.

Nelson rocked slowly in his seat. "I'm sure I heard the colonel say I'm to stay away until he makes a decision."

"There's no time to drop you off; you're stuck in the car. I'll note you tried to comply."

Chang turned into the Garden Ridge development. “We’re close to the Hubberts’ house.”

Nelson peered out the window. “He’s moving upscale. These homes are nice.”

“Yes, Wiggins said the father is a big lawyer in Wilmington. Try not to be too blunt. He just lost his daughter and thinks the whole thing was an accident.” If only they could view the scene without the family around. Nelson’s unconventional techniques might come across as inappropriate. He didn’t care what Byrd thought, but he didn’t want to add to a family’s pain.

The large brick house sat on a lush green lawn and immaculately landscaped yard. The doors of the three-car garage were open, and an officer along with an ambulance and its driver stood in the driveway. Inside the garage, Chang made out the back of a gold BMW.

They got out of the cruiser, and Ed Wiggins greeted them. Chang noticed he gave a respectful nod to Nelson.

Next to Wiggins Chang saw a short, squat man with a boxer’s nose and thick shoulders. He carried himself as though he walked into a strong wind. Must be the girl’s father. He stepped forward before anyone else could speak.

“Three cops to investigate an accident?” He stared at the notepad in Nelson’s hand. “He’s not a reporter, is he?” Cleary wore a lost look that reminded Chang of Jennifer Topper’s father.

Chang blocked the distraction and introduced himself.

“Mr. Rogers is consulting for the police. He’s not a reporter.” He could see he wouldn’t win the man’s trust easily.

“Mind if I stay with Heather?” Cleary asked. “She’s been through enough, don’t you think?”

Chang shot Wiggins a look and saw he took the hint. "It will be quicker if they work alone, sir. I'll be right there, and as soon as they're done we can come back."

Cleary seemed to wilt, but Chang knew it was temporary. They would have to work fast.

When Cleary went into the house, Wiggins returned.

Nelson ignored him and stared into the garage.

Chang quashed his annoyance. "What have we got?"

"The victim's on the garage floor," Wiggins said. "There's oil on the floor that she may have slipped on after she started her car. What it's supposed to look like, anyway. She falls, hits her head, and is overcome by the CO fumes. Get this: we dusted the key in the ignition, and it was clean. No prints at all. The father came home for lunch and found her. Be careful around him."

"How long can you hold him off while we take a look? We'll treat it like a homicide, but skip the suits. We don't want to upset him any more."

"Scene's been processed, but you'll see. I got him for now." Wiggins walked to the front door.

He stopped when Nelson spoke. "What was her name?"

"Heather Cleary. Her father is Ben."

They walked into the garage. Chang nodded to the ambulance driver, who was waiting for permission to remove the body.

Chang saw the shape under a sheet and noted the open door on the driver's side of the car. He could still smell the exhaust fumes, but the air was breathable. The garage looked compulsively tidy.

"Are you sure you're up to this?" Chang should have asked himself that question. The sight of a dead girl would evoke memories for both of them. Never mind. He'd let Jennifer Topper haunt him later.

When Nelson had had his breakdown in New York, the brass was all too happy to fix the blame on Chang. Anything to get a big shot like David Topper off their backs.

"Gotta be." Nelson's voice sounded distant.

He saw the puddle of oil on the floor. Chang lifted the sheet off the body and looked at the face last. He knew there wouldn't be green eyes, but he was wrong. Chang saw braces and bright green eyes. The floor tilted under his feet, and he thought he would fall. He bit down on his tongue and clung to the pain. He swallowed every drop of blood and forced his face to freeze.

At the end of the Jennifer Topper case, Nelson obsessed on the victim photos and had realized that every murdered girl wore braces. Killer was an orthodontist's assistant. A good catch, almost clever enough to save Jennifer…

The pain helped Chang refocus. They weren't braces. He saw a tongue stud in this girl's mouth. No metal bands. She had to be twenty, not a kid. Not anything anymore.

This girl's cheeks bore the vivid cherry color that was a hallmark of carbon monoxide poisoning. Chang saw swelling, snapped on gloves, and lifted her head. He felt distinctive lumps on the side and back of her head. *Lumps.*

"Feel this."

Nelson gloved up and put his fingers where Chang showed him. He whispered to the body. "You didn't bounce off the floor a couple of times after you slipped on oil that came from a bottle all the way across the garage."

Chang looked around the garage and needed to see no more to know that Wiggins and Nelson were correct. The girl was murdered.

CHAPTER 31

Flock Together

Dover, state police headquarters

Byrd sat in the empty conference room after Fargo finished his own impromptu post-meeting brief. His head pounded, and the aspirin remained stuck in his throat. The water seemed like too much trouble just now.

Should have known Spiker would try to set him up. Not too late to crimp those plans.

Patty knocked on the door glass, and the sound crashed into his skull.

"Colonel? If you're finished in here, Sergeant Foley's outside your office."

About time. "Thank you, Patty. We'll be a few minutes, so hold any calls."

* * *

"Close it." Byrd sat down and took a sip of water, which did nothing to dislodge the pills in his throat.

Foley got that hungry, expectant look Byrd had hated ever since Foley was a brat. Never mind, he's loyal. All that counts in the end.

"What's up, boss?"

"You didn't think Spiker was up to any hardball, eh? Here's a newsflash courtesy of Nick Fargo. He says Ms. Moral High Road sent Nancy Brand here to shanghai our favorite Asian detective so she can claim credit when they catch the nutcase we're after." Maybe Byrd would make that kid attorney general if all went well during the campaign.

"How do you figure? You hired him. He works for us." Clyde Foley always was better at taking orders than thinking.

"God damn it, wise up! When we hired Chang, she swooped in and had Nancy Brand trot him out like a trained monkey. We couldn't get any work out of him for two weeks while Spiker gloated over the new poster boy for diversity." Foley's face changed; Byrd got the whipped expression he wanted.

Bitch made it sound like it was her idea to hire him. Byrd swallowed. Pills felt like they were still there.

"Won't you get the credit for catching the killer?" Foley brushed lint off his uniform.

"Not if she can help it. She's going to let it slip that *she* pushed for that little freak, Rogers. Chang almost sold me. Christ, have you seen him? He's supposed to be some genius."

"Is he?"

"How should I know? He talks a good game. Maybe he is and maybe he isn't, but I'll tell you one thing he was right about."

"Yeah?" Foley leaned on Byrd's desk. He had that ambitious glint in his eye again. Good.

"We *will* solve the case with or without Rogers. Matter of fact, with or without Chang, which brings me to why you're here."

Foley stood straight. "Sir?"

"Sergeant, I'm not entirely convinced Detective Chang is up to the challenge of all the added pressure of a case like this."

"No?" Foley's hint of a smile told Byrd he followed.

"Keep a close eye on him. Watch for signs of stress, instability, and most of all, not playing by the rules. This is a big case. We can't afford to blow it if we have one of our own guys break down. We're a team."

And *I'm* in charge.

CHAPTER 32
Flash

Nelson gently released the head, yanked off the latex gloves, and scratched his scalp with both hands. Chang covered the body.

Nelson squatted near the corpse. He stared into space, put his hands over his head, and rocked. He began to moan, then to chant.

Chang watched but said nothing and hoped Cleary wasn't near the garage. Nelson had never gotten this loud before, but Chang didn't want to break in. Soon he could make out the words of the chant.

"…beforeIwake…IfIshoulddiebeforeIwake…IfIshoulddiebeforeIwake!" Nelson jumped up and swayed. He started to stagger out of the garage. Chang moved to catch him, but Nelson leaned on the back of the BMW and bowed his head next to the paper tag.

"Are you all right?"

Nelson snapped upright and stared out the open garage door.

"*Puja!*" The sound echoed in the garage. Nelson said it again, even louder, this time *at* the paper tag. "*Puja!*"

"Nelson?"

Nelson waved Chang off. "I'm fine."

The ambulance driver got out of his unit and approached Nelson, who ignored him.

Chang followed.

"I have him," Chang said over his shoulder to the driver. When he reached Nelson, he spoke to him in a low voice. "What?"

"In the car" Nelson never turned.

Chang *did* turn at the sound of a house door slamming. He saw Cleary gingerly step around his daughter and then storm out of the garage. Wiggins followed but made no move to stop him.

"What did he call her?" Cleary's face turned purple.

Chang intercepted him and kept his body between Cleary and the car. "Nothing. I think you may have misheard."

"I heard him shout something. What was it? Why does he need to yell? She can't hear him."

"Mr. Cleary, my partner means no disrespect." Chang steered Cleary away from the car. Chang started with the truth. "He had to leave active duty because of a condition."

"What's that?"

"They think it's a form of Tourette's. He's an unusually observant investigator, but as you have heard, his condition can present some difficulties." Chang wished he didn't have to make things up, but how could he give this man a rational explanation?

"They have medicine for that."

"Yes, sir, sometimes he misses a dose."

"What the hell is going on here?"

"We're not certain Heather's death was an accident."

"Not suicide. She slipped and fell." The man's face roiled with conflicting emotions. He grabbed Chang's arm, and his fingers felt like bird claws. "Wait… You mean murder? No one killed my Heather."

"Mr. Cleary, we owe it to your daughter to find the truth."

Cleary's added confusion made Chang wish he didn't have to fib.

He pointed at Nelson in the cruiser. "Keep *him* away from my daughter."

"Of course." Whatever Nelson was going to see already happened.

Cleary turned toward the house, and Chang glared at Wiggins. The big trooper's shrug told him he did all he could to delay Cleary, short of physical restraint.

Chang climbed into the driver's seat of the car and didn't speak. Inside, Nelson scribbled on a pad. Chang turned around, and Nelson stared with a pinwheel look in his eyes.

"Know what's funny about lemons? Puja, that's what! Our guy was making a joke with the lemon on Patel, and it was about puja! I know what he does for a living!"

"Slow down! Tell me who 'Puja' is." Chang grabbed Nelson's shoulders and shook him. Bird bones.

Nelson's head bobbled like a doll, and he finally met Chang's gaze. He spoke in a more coherent tone.

"Not who, but what. Puja is part of Hinduism. One aspect involves blessing mechanical items against bad influences. Used for household items. Blenders, ovens, and especially new cars!" Nelson grinned until he looked like a skull with a wig.

Chang tapped his reserves of patience. "Start with the bricks, then build me a wall."

"Okay, Hindus have blessing ceremonies for their cars for good luck. Sprinkle holy water and rice. Done by a priest called a *pujari*. End of the ritual is to place a lemon under each tire and run them over. Mr. Patel was a Hindu. The only Hindu, but I bet he shared something else with every victim."

Chang felt a gate swing open in his head. He looked out the window at the back of the BMW and stared at the T-tag. "You mean?"

"Picture the back of Midori's little car, with the footprints—try to remember."

"It was one of those new environmental type cars, and he'd just bought it... Hey!"

"Exactly. Another T-tag. Remember the shiny car in the Hubberts' driveway? Also a new car, I'm sure of it." Nelson had that giddy voice again.

"I think the Nguyens' son mentioned that his parents had just bought a car for the first time in about ten years," Chang said.

Nelson's words almost merged, and Chang thought of an engine at redline. "Want to bet Mr. Patel just bought one?"

Chang faced the front of the car. "Let's say that the common link between all the victims so far is that they bought a new car. What kind of car and from where?"

"Midori bought a Honda Insight; the Hubberts I think bought a Honda Accord. Do you remember what the Nguyens' son said they bought?"

"It might have been a Honda, too. This car is a Beamer. What else did you learn in the garage?" Chang twisted in the seat to face Nelson again.

"Obvious homicide. It was our guy, and this wasn't even a good fake."

Chang nodded. "You can tell from the lumps on her head she was hit multiple times, and the oil on the floor is after the fact. An owner who keeps the floors that clean would never leave a big oil puddle anywhere." Chang could feel the harmony with his partner's thoughts. "Amateur hour."

"Wiggins said no prints at all on the key, and I didn't see any gloves on her." Nelson doodled on the pad.

"No. But her father *wants* to believe it was an accident."

Nelson retraced his design repeatedly, and the pen tore through the top sheet. "Our killer is in the car business. That's the connection between victims. You'll see. The Nguyens and Patel will fit the pattern."

"I want to ease Mr. Cleary into the idea that this wasn't an accident, maybe let him sleep on it and try tomorrow to get his cooperation with a credit report. Do you think we'll lose anything by waiting a day?" Chang glanced out the window. They'd been a day late with Jennifer.

Nelson's breakthrough about orthodontists ended up getting delayed by red tape. They couldn't obtain the necessary search warrant for personnel records, and by the time they did and knew who to look for, Jennifer was dead.

"It would take that long to go over Cleary's head with a warrant, anyway," Nelson pointed out.

"You're right. Stay here. This is a crime scene now. We wouldn't want to upset the colonel." Chang got out of the car and walked back to the large house. Cleary stood with Wiggins on the front walkway.

"Mr. Cleary, we have everything we need for now. Is there a number where I can reach you tomorrow? I may have a couple follow-up questions."

Cleary appeared numb. He handed Chang a card. "You can reach me there, and the home number is on it, too."

"Thank you. By the way, I have to ask this. Your daughter didn't know anyone who might want to do her harm, did she?" Take advantage of Cleary's shock; he might close up later.

"Why would someone want to hurt my little girl?"

"Whenever there's an open investigation, we check every possibility. I'm very sorry for your loss. We can talk in the morning if that's better."

He spoke in a monotone. "Sure, I guess."

When Cleary was inside, Chang turned to Wiggins. "Thanks again for the heads-up. You didn't have to do that."

"I call them like I see them. That's my job." He lowered his voice. "Be careful. The brass has their ears on. I can't say too much."

Chang wasn't surprised. "You did plenty."

"That little guy has some kind of gift, doesn't he?"

"Something." Chang nodded.

"Word is, he's not welcome at any murder scenes. Be careful." Wiggins whispered.

"Don't mumble, Wiggins, I have no idea what you just said…and thanks."

* * *

On the way to the car, the ambulance driver stepped in front of Chang. "Does it look like a murder after all?"

"They'll let you know when they're ready for you." Chang brushed past and returned to the cruiser.

"We still have time to get to our notes and try to catch up with the Nguyens' son and maybe one of Mr. Patel's relatives," Chang said, feeling the blood pump.

"If we learn what I think we will, we have a busy evening ahead."

CHAPTER 33

When Life Gives You Lemons

Greenville, noon Monday

"Freebird!" Shamus shouted along with the soundtrack. The opening piano chords resounded in his small apartment. He sat at the kitchen table in his favorite boxer shorts and held the unloaded revolver. He liked this pair because they sported smiley faces and "Have a nice day!" encircled the elastic waistband. What a morning. Time for some mental dessert before work.

The song was the same, but this time he relived the thrill of taking down Patel, that grinding, maddening Indian.

What a rush! Fantastic. He wished he'd kept the security tape, but obviously that was out of the question. No problem, he wouldn't forget that experience anytime soon.

He swayed to the music and recalled how Patel had battered him during negotiations over a baseline Civic. The images played across his mind, and Shamus acted out Patel's pathetic protestations.

"Oh, no, no, no. I must have your best price. You can do better than that. I know. My cousin just bought the same car from Honda in New Jersey. I will pay you this." Shamus was proud of his imitation.

"You give me a good price, and I will bring my friends. You will sell many cars." All the Indians said that.

Shamus played with the lemons he kept in a bowl on the table. He wagged his finger just like Patel had.

"I don't want to play any more games. You go back to your man and come back with your best price, you know, or I am leaving. Tell him no more bullshit." It came out "booolshit."

Jake ripped into him. Shamus adopted Jake's rapid tone. "I need a closer, not an order taker!" Spittle flew from his mouth.

Shamus could still see the face clearly. The way Patel just started laughing. "I know you make plenty of money on this car. Okay, I go to Marlo and maybe they give me a good price." Shamus stood. The music filled the room.

Mr. Patel wouldn't need the free oil change Marlo threw in.

And his plan. So simple, so elegant. Hit him at work. Patel's home crawled with Indians day and night.

* * *

He'd known he needed to be quick because convenience store customers pop in at any time. He'd driven to the 7-Eleven around three in the morning.

When he'd yanked the door open, the tired-looking Indian reacted immediately. He spotted the chrome, snub-nosed revolver, and Shamus could tell Patel figured he was being robbed. Occupational hazard, right? An instant later his face registered recognition. At least their time together had left an impression.

Shamus shouted, "Best price!" in his finest Indian accent and fired away. More kick than the .22 and louder. Patel dropped like a marionette with his strings cut. Shamus remembered the electric thrill through his body that left him tingling. In that instant, he saw the lemon and had a moment of inspiration.

Shamus had seen Indian customers perform some sort of strange ceremony when they bought a car. It involved putting lemons under the tires of a new car and squashing them. He could still see the lifeless upturned face. Blood streamed out of the head. He raised his arm and brought the lemon down with all his strength onto the dead man's nose.

He'd watched the juice run down Patel's cheeks and mingle with the blood. He opened the cash register and cleaned it out. Made money off this guy after all.

* * *

Shamus rolled a lemon off the table and it dropped onto the old linoleum floor. He stopped it with one bare foot and then crushed the fruit with his heel. Juicy. He closed his eyes and shuddered with satisfaction.

The song built to its crescendo, and Shamus opened his eyes and dry-fired the pistol. "Best price! Best price!" The music covered his accented shouts. It was good to be alive.

CHAPTER 34

Naked Truth

Chang's house, Tuesday morning

Chang neared the summit of a cold mountain. The wind picked up and blew stray thoughts from his mind. Just a few more feet... A bell reached his ears, and his fingers slipped. Try again... The bell repeated loud enough to shatter the mountain.

And his meditation. He wiped the sweat from his forehead, uncrossed his legs, and heard himself groan when he stood up. The clock read five forty-five in the morning.

The doorbell rang again. Nobody came by this early.

Chang pulled on a robe and took the stairs two at a time. A loud crash of thunder played counterpoint to the insistent chime at the door. Rain drummed on the windows.

He stared through the peephole and saw a fisheye view of Nancy Brand. Her hair looked wet, plastered to her face, and water rolled down the open collar of her soaked shirt. Her cool professional veneer had vanished. She checked her watch and rang the bell again. Chang fumbled for the deadbolt.

"Detective," she said. "I hope I didn't...wake you."

It took him a moment to read between the lines. "I'm alone. I was working out." The rain continued. "You must be freezing." He took her hand and led her inside.

"I'm going to drip all over your floor. This won't take long..."

"Never mind the floor. This way." Chang walked up the stairs. He wasn't sure she'd follow until he heard the squeak of her shoes on the polished floor.

He led her into his bedroom and pointed to the bathroom. "The towels are fresh. I'll get you something dry to wear."

"You don't have to do that." Her voice sounded so low, not clear and self-assured like in the meeting.

Chang fished through his closet and picked out a cotton button-down shirt and a pair of sweatpants. Best he could do on short notice. Nancy was about the same size as Colleen, but her clothes were long gone.

Chang spoke through the bathroom door. "Whenever you're ready, *Ms.* Brand."

"Uh, yeah, that's awkward. First names okay with you?"

"Of course."

She opened the door a crack. "No peeking."

Chang handed the clothes through. Her fingers brushed his arm, and he resisted the urge to ignore her request.

* * *

In the kitchen Chang handed Nancy a steaming cup of tea. Her damp hair started to curl. Her bare feet tapped under the table. He wished Colleen had left a pair of slippers. "Is this business or personal?"

"I didn't phone so there'd be no record. Officially, I'm not here. Mr. Cleary just called Spiker and tore into her over the paper this morning."

"I haven't seen it yet." Chang never let it clutter his mind before meditation. "Wait, Cleary knows the governor's private number?"

"All three of them. He's got weight in this town, and she listens. She also just called Byrd and screamed at him. Cleary's daughter is all over the news. Somebody leaked it, and your fearless leader threw you under the bus."

"Huh?"

"Byrd told Spiker that you must be the leak. He wants to take you off the case."

Something didn't add up. "How does Byrd spin me as the leaker? The killer talks to Flannigan himself."

"Turns out Flannigan got scooped. The article this morning isn't his byline. Byrd ripped into Flannigan first thing, but the old guy not only denied it, but he's angrier than Cleary." Nancy gave a little smile.

"So there's a mystery source?" Chang began to get the picture.

"Right, but Byrd is taking the opportunity to use it against you."

"So why hasn't it happened? Byrd has my number. I should be fired now." Delaware was a smaller state but wore the same political plumage.

"Let's just say someone else the governor trusts put in a good word for you. The governor is frantic to see this case solved."

"Byrd's not?"

"Sure. With his own lackeys. You don't fit the profile, and it's no secret he's going to run against Spiker next year."

Ah, so. "How can I thank you for the honor of this information?"

"Some honor. You have to get to Cleary and calm him down. He was talking lawsuit, and Byrd told him the homicide designation was premature."

"Anyone with eyes knows it was murder."

"Cleary is blinded by grief. Byrd's using that."

"Okay, what do you need?"

"Talk some sense into Cleary pronto, then slip him this phone number."

Chang took the card. "It sounds like I'm getting kicked out of my own house."

"I have to go too, but maybe when there's more time I could return your clothes."

* * *

Chang stared at the *Daily Post* and waited for Nelson to pick up. He sounded sleepy.

"We have a situation."

"Another murder?"

"No, but it's not good. You haven't seen the paper this morning? Or listened to the radio?"

"Can't read in my sleep. I tried."

"We're on damage control this morning. The news about Heather Cleary's homicide, by the serial killer, is all over the place. Ben Cleary woke up the governor, after Byrd told him we leaked it."

"You talked to Byrd? He already knows I was there?"

"Maybe, but it doesn't matter. He wants to change the rules, we will too."

"How do you know this?"

"A secret admirer. I'll pick you up, and we'll go see Cleary. We have to convince him that his daughter was murdered."

"Who *did* leak?"

"Not on the phone. It's political now."

"I thought that's why I left New York."

"The classics never die."

* * *

Chang reached Nelson's in record time. Why weren't these cases ever about the crime? He thought Delaware would be different. But this was the first difficult case, and once again he was an outsider. Fate didn't recognize state lines...

Daisy bayed when he knocked, and Nelson opened the door.

"Do you have everything we pulled together last night?"

"Filed on the dining room table." Nelson slicked his hair down with a wet comb.

Byrd hadn't been the only busy one yesterday. Relatives of the Nguyens and Patel confirmed car purchases from Marlo Honda. Records showed the Hubberts and Midori bought there as well.

Now they had Heather, different brand, but a new car. They needed some information from Cleary to find out how she fit in. After they got Mr. Cleary to stop screaming *lawsuit.*

Chang filled in Nelson on the way. "So *somebody* exposes our case to the media, and Mr. Cleary wanders out about five this morning. He finds the early edition of the *Daily Post* in his driveway with a picture of his house on the front page and 'Serial Killer Strikes Again?' splashed across the top. He's upset, and being a lawyer, he wants to lash out."

"Byrd tells him you're to blame, and then Cleary hits up the governor?"

"Correct. Byrd figures this is enough to yank me off the case and the governor will back him up." Chang promised he'd worry about the colonel later. Right now he needed to focus.

"Feels like old times," Nelson said.

They got to the Cleary house just before seven. They weren't the first.

CHAPTER 35
Luck of the Irish

"This is what you call support?" Patrick Flannigan raised his voice as loud as he dared without a spasm of coughs. He shuffled back and forth in his bathrobe and held the morning paper. Both hands shook with fury.

"Pat, take it easy. It's a fast-moving story. We get tips too, you know." Yuri Krakow's accent grated. Flannigan thought he played it up to sound "exotic" to the locals. Got him to editor-in-chief, didn't it? He was Flannigan's boss, but not for long if things worked out.

"From the killer? You break this without me? I'm sorry, how much did you tell me our circulation was up?"

"Forty-two percent. We're all happy with your recent work. Do you want rose petals in your path? We're in the news business, and this story's bigger than just you."

Condescension from *him*?

"Who tipped you? The killer?"

"No, and never mind. We don't ask you how you get your information. And haven't we told the state police we'll stand by you with our entire legal staff?"

"You have. Considering that the source of this news calls me, don't you think you might want my input?" The lawyers would defend him as long as he sold papers. Screw the cops. He didn't know who the killer was, but it wasn't his job to figure it out, either.

"Calm down, Pat. Get in soon as you can. Of course we want you in on the follow-up stories."

With a little luck he wouldn't have to put up with this much longer. He thanked Krakow and hung up.

"And it's *Patrick*, you fucking Bolshevik!" He slammed the dead receiver and doubled over in a coughing fit. The noise almost drowned out the chirp of his cell phone. Maybe it was his lawyer. About time, for what he cost. He didn't trust the *Daily Post*'s legal buffoons for a minute.

He caught his breath. "Flannigan."

"You need to make up the news now?" Muffled voice. The source himself.

"You want my questions?" Flannigan scrambled for a pad. Guy never stayed on more than minute. Usually he told him where to pick up info and to hear Flannigan's new questions.

"Shut up. I don't know what you're trying to pull. That wasn't me, but I'll tell you who might be next."

Flannigan felt ice up his crooked spine.

"I didn't do that, believe me. I'm a straight shooter. Want to tell me your side?" He glanced at the kitchen clock.

"Just did."

"Cops don't think so. They say it's you." C'mon, open up. Give me something.

"They're too stupid. Someone gave them the idea. Next time you make the front page you'll be the story!" The call dropped. Fifty-three seconds.

Shit. He didn't know if the killer would calm down, but his timing couldn't be worse. Not when the *Times* showed interest in his work again. He was so close to a triumphant return to the city. Flannigan doubted the guy was serious about the threat. Besides, how could he ask for security when it would tip off that his pipeline to the killer was dry? Flannigan would show everyone he knew how to keep a secret.

CHAPTER 36
Columbo

Chang saw a WILM Newsradio truck outside the Clearys' house.

The rain had stopped, and the sky gave off a dull lead color. A tall reporter with slicked-back hair and a microphone hovered at the front door. Ace Duffy. Chang tried to call Cleary with his cell phone, but it was busy.

"Come on. Don't talk to this guy. Follow my lead." Chang got out of the car and marched toward the reporter. A short, rumpled producer intercepted him.

"Hey, we have a right to be here. We're just asking questions. You can't keep press away."

Chang whirled and towered over the man. "Your rights end at this man's property." Chang raised his voice. "If you don't want Ace under arrest for trespassing, get him out of here *now!*" Duffy watched the confrontation. Chang saw a curtain move inside the house. Good.

"You can't do this." The producer took a step back.

"These people have a *right* to their privacy. For the last time, get Duffy back and do your report from the street. Or I take him in. You too, if you interfere." Chang looked at his watch and then took out a pair of handcuffs from a leather holder on his belt.

"No need for the bracelets, Chang, just trying to do my job." Duffy pranced down the walk. "Who's that with you? A little puny for a trooper. He goes in the field with you, huh? Care to comment?"

Chang shook his head and noticed that the sly bastard had keyed on the mike while they were "just chatting."

"You left this on by mistake. Here, let me help you…" Chang gripped the microphone and felt Dragon-talons break off the plastic switch with his thumb. "Shoddy equipment…"

"You prick. You did that on purpose." Duffy held his ground and waved the broken microphone in Chang's face.

Chang dangled the handcuffs from his fingers. "Are you trying to obstruct a police officer?"

Duffy stepped aside. "Flannigan's right about you. Washed up…"

Chang blocked out the rest and turned away. He joined Nelson by the front door. He knocked, and it sprung open. Ben Cleary had huge bags under his eyes.

"I'd thank you for getting rid of him, but he wouldn't be here if not for you. Before I leave for court to file papers, would you care to explain to me how people like that got the impression Heather was murdered?" Chang and Nelson entered the opulent foyer. Cleary motioned them into the formal living room. Chang's eye for antiques spotted the collection of jade Buddhas in a glass case. No time to look closer, but he could tell the pieces were quality. He wondered if the Clearys' Western eyes saw beyond the monetary value.

Rose Cleary sat ramrod straight on the couch. She was a statuesque dark-haired woman. The hair was different, but he could swear she wore the same waxy grief mask that Jennifer Topper's mother showed in all those press conferences.

"I understand you're going to explain what happened." She sounded under control, but her glassy eyes said she was medicated.

"Mr. and Mrs. Cleary, first of all, I want to apologize on behalf of my entire department for failing to prevent information about this case from going public prematurely. I can assure you that Mr. Rogers and I didn't say a word."

"But why would the papers print lies?" Rose turned her head as though she had a stiff neck.

"We're all upset about the leak, but the facts would have come out eventually." Chang kept his eyes on Rose. Her pain told him this was not the time for a fiery avenger.

Cleary took his wife's hand. "What are you saying?"

"These reporters, while insensitive, aren't wrong. I'm sorry, but your daughter *was* murdered."

"We went over this. It was an accident!" Cleary's voice bounced off the walls, and Rose flinched. Chang leaned forward and spoke to her in his most gentle tone.

"Mrs. Cleary, I see what a tidy house you have. Even your garage was spotless, and yet there was a puddle of oil on the floor. Would any of you leave such a mess?"

"Well, no, but you should see her room." Rose wore a vacant smile.

"She would have no reason to touch the oil can, would she?"

"No, but…" Cleary paused. "I didn't want to say anything…" He cleared his throat. "She used drugs sometimes. Maybe she didn't know what she was doing. I'm not stupid. I wondered why she would start the car with the garage door closed. Hell, she might have driven right through it if she didn't slip." He started to sob and turned it into a cough.

"Mr. Cleary, your daughter didn't slip. The oil was poured on after the fact. Whether she happened to be high wouldn't have made a difference. Also…" Chang looked from one to the other.

"What?" Cleary said.

"I saw her body. When someone slips and hits their head, there's one distinct impact spot. I found at least three contusions, maybe more. She was struck several times with a blunt object."

Rose made a sound like a kettle on full boil. Her wail ripped though Chang's professional veneer and forced him to look away. Before he did, he saw her mask dissolve and she covered her face with both hands.

Cleary hugged her, and Chang wished they could let them grieve in private. He felt like a voyeur.

Cleary looked up after several agonizing minutes. "What were the other facts?"

Chang felt some hope rise along with the sadness that came from close contact with victims' families.

"We checked the key in the ignition and found no fingerprints."

"What's odd about that?" Cleary said.

"Unless Heather always wore gloves when she started her car, we would expect to see at least traces of her prints.

Instead, we found nothing. The key was wiped clean." Chang could see the concept begin to take hold.

"Who?" Her jaw set, and she looked like she was in the room for the first time.

"We hoped you might help us find out who. I'm going to ask for your trust."

"After this morning?" Cleary's face flushed.

"I'm asking anyway. My partner will tell you why. Something that I can't." Chang moved out of earshot.

He saw Nelson explain their theory about the new-car link. Cleary looked furious.

"Detective Chang, why didn't Byrd tell me this? What the hell is going on here?"

Chang took Cleary aside. "Officially, I can't say." Chang pressed one of Nancy's cards into Cleary's palm. "Call the number; you'll have the answer." Chang led Cleary back to the couch.

"Was Heather looking at any other types of cars, like Hondas?"

"We gave her money, but we don't know where she went." Cleary spoke, and Rose stared down.

"Once she picked a car, you would take care of the payments?"

"It would come out of her allowance," Rose said. "But yes."

"Would the deposit and paperwork be in your name?"

"No, I insisted it all be in hers; we just helped her with the finances," Cleary said.

"Could we have your permission to run a copy of Heather's credit, so we can see where else she might have looked?"

"No. We don't need her name dragged through the press any more."

Chang wasn't surprised by the lawyer's reflexive response. Could get what he wanted anyway, but right now he needed to show deference.

"Mr. Cleary, you could help us get closer to whoever did this. If we have to wait, the killer could be after someone else's daughter." Sometimes the truth cut like a scalpel.

Cleary seemed to crumble. "Just try to keep it quiet and stay away from anything about the drugs. I don't want her remembered that way." He signed the waiver and wrote down her social security number.

Chang walked to the front door and peeked out the glass in the frame.

"The area is clear for now. Mr. Cleary, if you'd like, I'll have a unit stay with you today and keep the media off your property."

"I'd appreciate that, Detective." Cleary looked ten years older than he had the day before. Chang made the call.

"He'll be here in ten minutes. Until then, keep your door locked and let the answering machine screen your calls."

* * *

Chang called in a request to run a credit report on Heather. Nelson and Chang sat in his car while they waited.

"I was going to run a check on her for priors, anyway."

"How soon?"

"I'll get the arrest record read to us on the radio. The credit material should be on my desk when I get there."

Chang called in to dispatch, and they promised a response in a few minutes.

Nelson fidgeted in his seat. “Why haven’t we moved?”

“Think. Is there any chance the killer might return to the scene of the crime and finish off the rest of the family?”

“Oh. We stay until backup comes?”

“I didn’t want to scare these poor people any more than necessary, but we don’t budge until they’re covered.”

Back in New York, Chang always had to remind Nelson about his own personal security. A couple of times during some tense investigations he’d followed Nelson home, unobserved, just to make sure the wrong people didn’t try to harm the precinct’s top investigator.

“If he was after the parents, they’d be dead with Heather. I think he added his signature even though he was trying to make it look like an accident. Couldn’t resist,” Nelson said, and then he began to look at his notes.

“What was it this time?”

“If my theory holds, the car itself, since it was the real murder weapon. I’ll know for sure after we get a look at the credit report.”

A dark blue twin to Chang’s cruiser pulled alongside.

“Howdy.” Steve D’Agostino greeted Chang across the driver’s side windows. He looked like he still wore shoulder pads under his uniform, but his football days were long over.

Chang briefed him.

“No problem, man.” D’Agostino smiled over at Nelson, who gave him a shy nod. “Hey, Columbo, you forgot your raincoat!” D’Agostino had a deep laugh.

CHAPTER 37

Suspended Animation

"One-one-two, this is dispatch."

"Go ahead, dispatch."

Chang always marveled at how mechanical dispatchers could sound; he almost didn't recognize Irma over the radio, but he knew her from around headquarters.

"Dispatch" told them that Heather pleaded no contest twice for possession of marijuana, had several speeding tickets, and recently was charged with failure to control her vehicle in a single-car accident.

"Does the report say what kind of car?" Nelson said.

"Irma, what type of vehicle was in that crash?" Chang relayed.

"One-one-two, please observe proper radio procedure."

Chang used his most formal tone. "Correction. Dispatch, please advise if report indicates make and model of single vehicle."

"One-one-two, thank you. Report indicates vehicle was a 2002 Honda Accord coupe, license plate Delaware 6523."

"Thank you, dispatch."

"Ten-four."

Chang replaced the microphone. “It doesn’t sound like she was into anything serious, does it?”

Nelson doodled on his pad. “Possession counts, nothing heavy.”

Chang turned into the headquarters parking lot. “So, she wrecks her new Honda, then her parents spring for a BMW.” Chang pulled in next to a dumpster.

“Do you have to park so close? It’s a war between the vegetarians and the carnivores in there. Ugh.” Nelson rolled up the window.

“Use it as cover. Wait a minute after I’m gone and then go. Byrd’s upset enough as it is. He doesn’t need to see us come in together.”

* * *

“You’re late.”

Chang turned and saw Foley. Pressed uniform and stupid grin. “I was in the field.”

“You’re supposed to call it in. I don’t have it on the board.”

“Nobody was there to take the call, and I was on the move.”

“We have a machine.”

“Foley, is this going somewhere?”

“You tell me.” Chang caught the smirk, and the guy pointed to the interoffice memo folder on top of what had to be the credit report for Heather. The folder bore the colonel’s stamp. Another log across the road.

Chang needed to get his mind serene before he confronted the memo. He grabbed the side of his desk to line it up for meditation.

At first he thought the desk was caught on something, but then he realized the legs were bolted to the floor. He opened the drawer where he kept his fountain and chimes. Gone.

Foley. Toad. Petty bureaucrat. Just kept pushing…

The guy stood at the end of the room with his hands on his hips like a scolding old woman. Chang covered the distance and watched Foley's smirk dry up. Foley backed up until the edge of a desk bent him backwards. Chang smelled his fear.

He loomed over Foley and spoke through gritted teeth. "Give me my…property." Chang almost said "wind chimes" but realized the worm would laugh. Sweat rolled down his face onto Foley, who recoiled.

Chang's vision sharpened, and he saw Foley's pores fill and heard the flutter of his heart…like prey…

Foley squeaked like a mouse. "Hit me and I'll prosecute."

Chang felt his own heart gallop and realized the Dragon wanted out. It stared at Foley. The scaled head began to wriggle through the bars of its cage… Chang tore his gaze away and concentrated on restraining it.

"Yeah, that's what I thought. I heard you would back down." Foley looked relieved, and a trace of his smile resurfaced. He pointed at the paper still in Chang's hand. "Don't you have bigger rice to fry?"

The Dragon pulled back, for now. Chang tore open the memo. Report at once… Pithy.

* * *

"Close the door."

Chang did.

"I know that you brought Rogers to crime scenes after I specifically said not to."

"Sir, the last one we didn't know..."

Byrd glared at Chang. "Don't interrupt me again. That's insubordination. Rogers's contamination of the crime scenes is good enough to boot you off the case, but I can't do that. Got a call from Governor Spiker's office. Seems Cleary, all upset this morning, is now so enthusiastic about helping that he's joining a press conference this afternoon with the governor and yours truly."

Nancy was good.

Byrd's voice rose. "Not only that, but I've been told to expect representatives of the...'wack' something." He pawed through a sheaf of papers. "The WAACs and the CIA Wilmington."

"WAACs and CIA, sir?" Chang didn't have to pretend to be confused.

"Forgot to renew your membership? The Wilmington Asian American Community and, for good measure, the Community of Indian Americans will join them. They'll be front and center to grill me on why we didn't expand our efforts until the murderer started killing white people."

Nancy was *very* good.

"Don't look so surprised, Chang."

"Sir, I didn't know about any press conference. I met with Mr. Cleary this morning when I saw the paper. We were following up as related to the case." *We.* Byrd pounced on the slip.

"Those pronouns can be tricky, can't they? Chang, you're a good cop, but you don't understand how we do things in Delaware, do you?"

He understood perfectly.

"We're a big small town here. We're all a family of sorts, and that means this state is different."

Where was this going?

"Part of being in a family means you look out for one another. Take Foley, for example. We trust each other."

"With all due respect, sir, he's your cousin."

"There you go again. That's your problem. You don't see the big picture."

"Sir, the big picture is that we have a killer on the loose." Even Shu would lose it with this man.

"We'll catch the killer. Rogers said so. I don't know what you pulled to get the governor on your side, but just because you're still on the case doesn't mean you can do whatever you want. Catch this nut, but if you don't go by the book, I'll have your shield and weapon, and maybe file charges."

Chang noticed Byrd's head. It looked like a red bowling ball. "Of course, sir."

"You roped me into this stupid presser; maybe you should join me."

"Sir, I'm on the trail. I don't have time to…"

"If you need time, I could always have you suspended. Like I did Rogers… Oops, there goes the surprise." Byrd grinned.

"Suspended?"

"Apparently you both forgot Rogers is an employee of the state police. His attendance has been spotty lately, and he's been seen interfering with my best investigator. I suggest you learn to play ball, or his suspension might become permanent."

"Some team." Forget sharing the news about Nelson's breakthrough. Byrd would probably leak it anyway.

"If all goes well next year when I'm elected governor, I can see to it he gets a nice job with the department of tourism. The director is another cousin of mine."

"The one who came up with the slogan 'Delaware—We Were Here First'?"

"That's him. I hope you don't disappoint me, Chang. Catch this guy, but remember who you work for."

* * *

Chang returned to his desk. He could feel Foley watching him from across the room. Nelson walked onto the floor and shuffled over to Chang.

Chang looked at his friend. "You heard?"

Nelson waved an official-looking piece of paper. "Effective today for an 'indefinite period,' it says."

Chang felt his face flush, but he refused to show his emotion while Foley leered at them.

"I'll take you home."

"Are you sure?"

"Byrd'll need something bigger to remove me, so he can embarrass the governor. Until then I've been spared. Your suspension was a warning to me. I'm sorry."

"Not your fault. I'm a tool, that's all."

* * *

At Nelson's place they looked through the report on Heather Cleary.

"Does this say she put down four different deposits?" Nelson pored over the printout.

"Yes. Look at the detail on her credit card. She charged five hundred dollars each to Diamond State Lexus, Patriot Motors, and Marlo Honda. Interesting. Why would she buy four cars and then ditch three of them for the BMW?" Chang tried to block out the bizarre events of the day and focus.

"Couldn't make up her mind?"

"Maybe. She bought *two* Hondas. First a deposit down at Patriot, and then a day later she charged one to Marlo. After Marlo, she put money on a Lexus. Two days after that, she bought the BMW." Chang felt dizzy. "In the morning we can begin with Marlo, where all but one of the cars were sold."

"We?" Nelson looked worried.

"Dealers don't know you aren't official."

Nelson smiled. "My schedule seems to have opened up."

"You'd think for once we'd get one where we only fight the bad guys." Chang knew he wouldn't get much sleep. The trail was warm.

He'd stop by to see Shu. Maybe he could help him relax.

CHAPTER 38

Three's a Crowd

Wilmington, Patriot Motors, Tuesday evening

Shamus wanted trumpets to announce the arrival of Myrtle the Timid. Due any minute now, she told him she'd bring a friend to help. The more the merrier.

She better appreciate that he was here on his day off.

"Famous Shamus on overtime! Tonight's the night? Your girlfriend's really coming in to talk turkey?" Jake clapped him on the shoulder.

"I'd say it's time to consummate."

"You hung in there; I'm proud of you. That's salesmanship. You've earned this one; go and take it." Jake walked away, and Hank sidled up.

"I don't know why you put up with her," Hank said. "She's unbelievable. I'd have told her to hit the bricks a long time ago, man." Hank waved his thumb like a hitchhiker.

The sun set, and Myrtle arrived in a shiny red Dodge pickup escorted by a middle-aged black man with gray hair and a strong-looking frame. His face could have been dark granite for all the warmth it held. Myrtle smiled and nodded to Tommy and Jake, who stood near the front of the showroom.

"Good evening, Shamus! I want you to meet Larry Stiles. He's going to help me out."

She wore her Sunday best for the occasion.

"Nice to meet you, Mr. Stiles." Shamus extended his hand, and the man shook it without enthusiasm. Stiles didn't make eye contact.

"You too." Stiles spoke to the floor.

"Larry worked with my husband at the machine shop in Newark before he died."

"Oh, I was sorry to hear about her loss; he sounded like a good man." Shamus hoped to find some common ground.

"Uh huh." Stiles looked around the showroom, and his eyes lingered on the little hybrid.

"I see you're looking at the Insight. Those are neat cars, and if you want another vehicle to commute to work in, they'd certainly cost less to run than your truck."

"Not interested in a Honda. I like my truck and have a short commute. Besides, why come all the way here when I could just go to Marlo? I'm here for Myrt." He glowered at Shamus.

"He lives right near the shop, over in Carpenter Woods. Almost walking distance."

The mention of Marlo nudged up Shamus's blood pressure. He needed to get things back on track.

"Let's have a look at the buyer's order, shall we?" Shamus reviewed every feature and option. Stiles looked bored. "Have I left anything out?"

"No, Shamus, that's what I want, in the light blue. I'm ready to talk about the price."

Sure you don't want to think about it another five or ten years?

Shamus played up the discount and slid the buyer's order toward Myrtle. She said nothing and looked over at Larry, who rolled his eyes. "Boy, you must think we're simple! That ain't no discount!" Stiles raised his voice. "You think I don't know anything?"

Shamus knew most of the other salesmen were trying to look busy, but they were listening intently.

"Sure it is, this is a…"

Stiles cut him off. "Not here to waste time. Let you in on a little secret. I happen to know a woman who bought an Odyssey right here last week and got seven hundred and fifty dollars off, so don't go starting with that 'no discount' stuff. You need to do a whole lot better that that, son."

"That lady lives next door to the owner, so she got an exception. Tell you what. If I could get Jake to match that discount, would we have a deal?"

Myrtle seemed detached from the process, so Shamus looked and talked to Larry. This wasn't the plan at all!

"Hell no! We need *at least* fifteen hundred dollars off the van. Minimum."

"Myrtle, Mr. Stiles, I appreciate you want a good deal and to protect your friend. Nobody sells these vans for that much off."

"I don't care. You get in there and tell your boss to knock another fifteen hundred dollars off that price, and maybe we'll have something."

"Let me understand. Now you're saying you want an additional fifteen hundred dollars off, on top of the original five-hundred-dollar discount?"

"No, on top of the seven hundred and fifty. Who do you think you're trying to run this by?" Stiles snorted laughter at him.

Myrtle sat like a stone and refused to come to his rescue.

"Mr. Stiles, I can't go into my manager's office with anything close to a request like that. There's no point."

"I believe you heard me. Get in there and get me that price so we can start negotiating for real, or else we'll go somewhere else." He folded his thick arms across his chest.

"Then we're done." Shamus heard himself speak. It took all his concentration to sound calm.

"I'm sorry to have taken so much of your time, Myrtle. I told you how popular these vehicles are, and you will not find them at any dealership in the country for that price."

They got up and walked out without another word. Myrtle never even looked back.

Several salesmen looked at him. His head felt like it would pop. He smiled, shook his head, and walked by Hank.

"You sure called that one," Shamus said. "They were out of their minds. Glad I didn't spend the money ahead of time." He tried for a "can't win 'em all" tone.

"I told you," Hank commiserated, "don't waste your time with the crazy people, they're unbelievable. I mean, I don't know what universe they're living in, man. You can't discount enough to make them happy. So I don't try."

Shamus walked into Jake's office. Get it over with.

"Shamus, what was that? What happened?"

He explained their demands and how Stiles knew about the owner's neighbor.

"This is a small town; next thing you know everybody and his brother will want that discount."

Shamus only heard enough of Jake to hold up his end of the conversation. He felt consumed by the need to balance the account with Myrtle and Larry. Soon. Then again, what about Heather? Press found out too quick. Maybe he should lay low. People might remember Myrtle… The icehouse popped into his mind. He could smell Gran's liniment oil.

"…think there's any point to following up? I mean, how did you leave it with them?" Jake broke into his thoughts, but now his voice sounded like Gran's.

"I left it with them leaving." He felt more pressure in his head. Not *now*, Gran. "When Marlo laughs them out of the store, we probably have a shot." Shamus felt like he was floating above his body. He watched himself hold a coherent conversation with Jake.

"You're taking this well," Jake said. "I'd be pretty hot."

He heard her ring the cowbell. It matched the pulse in his temples.

"A tantrum won't make us any money, and they aren't being reasonable. I hope they come around. For now, I don't have much choice but to file it under 'shit happens' and move on, right?" Shamus needed to get out of there.

"Too bad we don't give medals for keeping your cool… oh my God!"

Shamus felt a gush of fluid on his upper lip. In an instant, he reunited with his floating self. He cupped his hand, and it filled with blood. Drops spotted paperwork on Jake's desk.

Jake scrambled in a desk drawer, and Shamus tilted his head back. He swallowed blood and felt his gorge begin to rise. He accepted a wad of tissue and covered his nose. He felt dizzy.

"Can you make it to the bathroom? Should I call 911?" Jake sounded like Jake again. Shamus waved him away and took a fresh bunch of tissue. He threw the soggy batch in the trash and walked onto the showroom toward the one-stall restroom.

The other salesmen gawked.

His nose stopped bleeding, but he looked like he'd been shot. He wiped crusty streaks of blood off his face, and his head cleared. He got Gran's message.

Shamus let the negotiation replay in his head. He wadded up some paper towels and screamed his frustration into them. The paper muffled the sound. When he looked up at the mirror, his face was distorted with rage.

Sure, he'd file it under "shit happens" all right. Then he'd put it under his new "shit happens *back*" file.

What was left of his caution lay in a blood-soaked wad in Jake's office.

CHAPTER 39

Early to Bed

Shamus didn't remember much of the rest of his shift. When it was over, he drove in the direction of his apartment just long enough to fool anyone who saw him leave.

He headed toward Newark, Delaware. Myrtle, bless her heart, mentioned that Larry Stiles lived in Carpenter Woods, but not exactly where. No problem. He had all night.

He already knew where Myrtle lived. The artist community of Arden, located in the northern part of the county. Bunch of hippies. Residents leased the land they lived on. No one actually owned their property. So communal.

Shamus drove along the rows of small houses. No garages, and Shamus figured Stiles for a homebody. Soon enough, Shamus spotted the bright red pickup. Just in case, he drove through the rest of the development. Stiles was the sole owner of a new red Dodge model. Nice truck. Shamus hoped he hadn't paid too much for it.

The lights in the house were out, and Shamus was thankful Myrtle was such a blabbermouth. According to her, Stiles had lived alone since his wife passed several years ago.

"You'll be with her soon, Larry, my man," Shamus said aloud inside his car. He drove away and pointed his old car north. He needed to get to bed, too. Big day planned tomorrow.

CHAPTER 40

Out Like a Champ

Greenville, Wednesday morning

Shamus awoke early and pulled on his painter's coveralls. He packed a large, zippered canvas bag. He consulted the DART bus schedule and finished eating folded toaster-waffles over the sink. He called work and croaked a message for Jake that he wouldn't make it in today.

He parked in the Newark train station lot and went to the bus stop to wait. He wore his cap and sunglasses like any other hard-working painter. The bus arrived, and Shamus saw he should reach Carpenter Woods in plenty of time to beat Stiles home for lunch.

He hoisted the heavy pack and got off at his stop. Despite the pleasant temperatures, Shamus was dripping sweat by the time he reached Stiles's house. The street was quiet, and there was no sign of the nicest red truck in all of Carpenter Woods.

On one side of the house Shamus saw a ground-level window that wasn't visible from the front. Perfect. A small white tarp muffled the sound of broken glass nicely. After he cleared the stray fragments, he covered the bottom of the frame and wriggled in. He checked his watch again and saw that it was a little after eleven o'clock. Better hurry.

He pulled on his gloves and looked around. The basement was neat, and in addition to laundry machines he could see a nice set of woodworking tools.

He went up the stairs and listened. The heft of the revolver in his waistband gave him reassurance. Nobody home. Shamus checked the path Stiles would take. The front door opened into a narrow hallway. To the left a coat closet, and to the immediate right the living room, where he could see a comfortable couch and a huge television. The TV must have been added after the demise of the lovely wife. A guy's setup all the way, and no expense spared on the audio.

Inside the room, he saw framed photos of a woman who had to be the missus and a baseball bat on a stand. It was autographed by the entire world-champion Phillies team from 1980. He found the remote and turned on the television. It drew power with a low hum, and the surround-sound speakers crackled to life. He hit the mute button and unhooked the wire that controlled the feed to all the speakers. He took it off mute and cranked the volume all the way up. Green bars crawled silently across the screen. He switched the set off and reconnected the speakers.

Shamus slipped the remote into a pouch on the front of his coveralls and picked up the bat.

* * *

Shamus's heart jumped when he heard the distinctive V8 rumble of Stiles's truck. He grabbed the bat, tiptoed down the hall, and opened the closet door to duck inside. He jammed himself in between a mass of coats. No time to wriggle behind them, but he just managed to get the door closed.

He heard keys in the lock and slid the bat down his side, the shaft held up by layers of coats. The smell of mothballs and faint perfume wrapped around his face. Shamus reached inside the coveralls for the comfort of the revolver and heard the lock turn. He needed to pee, but it would have to wait.

The door squeaked. He heard Stiles sigh. Shamus braced himself. The seconds dragged by, and his urge to piss grew stronger. At last he heard and felt the big man's footsteps go down the hall to the kitchen. The clank of the keys on the kitchen table was a relief.

Shamus opened the closet door just enough to poke the remote toward the living room. He took a deep breath and pressed the button.

Powerful system! The speakers blasted sound through the house.

"Have you been hurt in an accident? Then you need a lawyer! Call Schick and Spivey at area code three-zero-two…" Shamus closed the door to a crack.

"What the hell?" Shamus barely made out Stiles's voice, but he felt his footsteps down the hall. A jingle for dog food began. Shamus saw Stiles round the corner to turn off the television. Now! Now!

"Where the hell is the damn remote?" Stiles's back was to the closet. The chorus of happy puppies drowned out the creak of the door. Stiles moved toward the TV. Shamus held the bat above his head and charged. Stiles turned a second before Shamus pivoted his body and swung for the fences. He aimed at the man's head.

"Here's one from the team!" Shamus whooped. Energy supercharged his arms and shoulders.

In the instant before the bat connected, Shamus saw recognition along with the surprise. Beautiful. The shock of the impact ran up his arms. Stiles went down hard, and a fan of blood sprayed the opposite wall. Shamus hovered over his vanquished opponent and felt the adrenaline thump through his body. He beat a bigger, much stronger man this time. What a rush!

His ears began to ache, and he realized the TV was still blasting. He lowered the volume and left the set on to provide some background noise.

Blood ran from Stiles's skull, and the man didn't budge. Good enough. Chalk up another favor to the world.

"Okay, big man, we've got some more business together." Shamus grabbed one arm and started to drag Stiles toward the stairs. The head left a trail where the bat had struck him. Jeez, he was heavy! Shamus began to sweat again, and soon he felt winded. Stiles's body was only a third of the way up the stairs, but Shamus had to rest.

"Damn! You're still a pain, you know that?" This wasn't going to work. Shamus stood to think of another option. His heart skipped a beat when he felt a hand grip his leg.

"Uhhh." Stiles's eyes fluttered, and his fingers tightened around Shamus's ankle. He kicked and pulled away. He managed to free his leg but lost his balance. Shamus tumbled down the stairs and felt pain flare on his side. His heart hammered in his chest, and he rolled over in time to see Stiles rise up. Shamus scurried backwards.

"Sonofabitch." Stiles sounded drunk, but he could walk.

Shamus stared. He'd crushed the man's head—he knew he did. Too late, he realized he left the bat near the bottom of the stairs. Stiles saw it too.

"Out...my...house..." Stiles picked up the slugger. His own blood marked the wood.

Panic engulfed Shamus. The man looked enormous from his position on the floor. The bat loomed like a telephone pole.

"Scared now..." Stiles staggered closer and lifted the bat.

Shamus fumbled at his waistband. He wasn't going to make it. He groped for the handle of the revolver, found it, but the bat was already swinging down at him. He tugged at the pistol and shut his eyes.

The boards next to Shamus's head jumped from the impact.

"Goddammit. Hold still," Stiles wheezed.

Shamus snapped his eyes open and saw Stiles lose his footing and collapse on top of him. The weight forced the air out of his lungs, and Shamus couldn't scream when Stiles's hand groped for his eyes. His right hand was pinned, but he could still move his finger.

The shots sounded nothing like when he fired on Patel. Stiles's belly muffled the blasts, and Shamus squeezed off every round. Something like a cross between a scream and a groan escaped the big man's lips, and Shamus felt his gun hand grow warm with the flow of blood. He wriggled out from under the still form and took a minute to catch his breath.

His side hurt, but he didn't think anything was broken. Joy rose in his chest. He won! Euphoria pushed away the pain. His white painter suit was now two-tone, and his arm was drenched in crimson. The odors that mixed in the hallway were the smell of victory.

He glanced at the stairs. No way.

"All right, change of plan, Larry. I hope you don't mind. Adapt and overcome, right, Mr. Protector?"

Stiles raised no objections, and Shamus found it much easier to drag him on the floor. The belly wounds leaked a wide red swath all the way to the basement door. The bloody head made a thump, thump, thump sound down the stairs.

Too bad he couldn't tell Flannigan about this. He wanted to gloat, but he didn't need the munchkin anymore to tweak that stupid cop, Chang.

He reached into his bag and pulled out a kitchen trash bag, then picked up a small handsaw. He glanced around and smiled. He returned the small tool and selected a large bow saw off the wall.

"Don't worry, you won't feel a thing."

CHAPTER 41

Arts and Crafts

Shamus whistled the whole way up to Arden. He enjoyed the throb of the V8 in Stiles's truck, and he was impressed with the commanding view. He wore fresh coveralls and took care to keep his speed under control. Wouldn't do to get pulled over now.

Almost quarter past two. Myrtle taught a pottery class in West Chester, just over the state line in Pennsylvania. She would probably get home by eight o'clock, which didn't leave him much time. He shouldn't rush great art, but he'd just have to do his best.

He parked the truck in the winding gravel driveway. It was an old farm house with a large garage extension Myrtle used as her studio. Myrtle confessed to being nervous sometimes because she didn't think her neighbors could see or hear what went on at her property. With her husband gone, she sometimes felt like it was too secluded for her. Shamus had told her to treasure her privacy.

He borrowed a pair of bolt cutters from Stiles and used those to let himself into her studio from the outside. He saw another entrance connected to the house. On one side she kept finished works, which included some stunning pieces on custom-built shelves. A large worktable took up the adjacent wall.

Aha! The Saturn-brand octagonal kiln. Shamus recognized it at once. Myrtle had talked his ear off about it one day.

She'd taken advantage of his manners by giving him chapter and verse on the thing's operation. He knew it could reach temperatures upwards of two thousand degrees. It also had a timer that would tell it when to shut off. He didn't remember everything, of course, but he'd gotten the gist.

He plopped the canvas bag onto the table and tried to recall art classes from long ago in Ohio. He checked her supply of porcelain glazes and found one he thought to be a good choice. "Toreador Scarlet" sounded suitable. Once he mixed the glaze, he set the kiln's timer.

* * *

Shamus marveled at the beauty of the sunset. All this art and his own creative effort put him in a poetic spirit. He even turned his face into a canvas of sorts when he borrowed some foundation to cover the scratches from Stiles down his cheek. She had plenty of painkillers, but Shamus stuck to the over-the-counter type for his ribs. No time for sleep now.

He waited for Myrtle in the main house. Couldn't stay in the studio. His hands itched from the gloves, but he bore the discomfort like a professional.

Just for fun, he checked Myrtle's mail table but didn't see a cell phone bill. That was good. Neither did he see any sign of firearms. She certainly didn't seem the type. He knew she didn't trust banks. She'd squirreled away close to twenty thousand dollars cash in a shoe box in her closet. Score!

When headlights splashed across the living room wall, he ducked. She would see the truck and assume Larry was here. Shamus giggled from behind a couch, pistol at the ready. The door opened, and she came in alone.

"Helloo? Larry, are you here? Larry? What's burning?" The musty old rugs absorbed the sound of her voice. The tick of the grandfather clock in the hallway served as a counterpoint to her questions.

Shamus heard her put her purse down and then sniff the air again. "Ugh!" She moved toward the garage door that led to her studio. Shamus was used to the smell by this time, but it *was* pungent. Wait till she opens the door! He was glad the kiln shut down a couple hours ago, but it was probably still warm.

"Larry, are you in the studio? What have you got in the kiln? Something in there is burning. Larry?" She opened the door.

Shamus tried not to laugh. He heard a final, "Oh my goodness!" when she opened the door and got the full effect.

He heard her run across the room, and then he tiptoed over to the doorway. Yeesh! It really stunk in there! He saw Myrtle, with her back to him, put on long, heat-resistant gloves. She picked up the tongs near the kiln and lifted the lid. Shamus could see a fresh pall of smoke rise along with intense heat shimmers.

"Oh! What in the world got in here? Larry, what did you do?"

She reached in with the tongs to wrestle out the object. Shamus was impressed. She was stronger than she looked.

He could hear the crackle across the room when the thick glaze, still hot from the firing, cooled unevenly in the open air. Despite the rough treatment and his novice stature, he thought the final result turned out well.

Myrtle dropped the tongs and staggered back. She grabbed the wall for support. The bright red mass stared back. It smoldered but was still recognizable as a human skull. The moisture from it had produced radical flaws in the glaze that was so over-applied it puddled to form its own glassy base.

Shamus leaned against the doorframe. "I wasn't sure if I'd get a nice shrunken head, or a glossy red statue."

Myrtle screamed and looked over at him.

He walked into the converted garage. "The way it turned out, I guess you could go either way. I thought maybe a hood ornament to go on his truck, but maybe you could do a shelf for him? I don't know. You're the expert."

"Shamus, what did you do?" Her voice quivered.

"A decent job for my first try. You shouldn't be so critical. I'm self-taught, you know." He moved closer. She seemed petrified, but he didn't count her out just yet.

"What do you want?"

"Before we get to that, come over here. You're a little too handy with those tongs."

Myrtle raced for the outside door. Shamus smiled. There wasn't going to be a chase through the woods. The door was locked tight. Myrtle jiggled the handle to no avail.

No way out but through him. First flight, then fight. Good for her.

She picked up the tongs again and came at him. Before she took two steps, he drew his revolver and pointed it at her nose.

"You know, if you'd stuck up for me a little yesterday, you might be looking forward to a future of porcelain wishes and caviar dreams. But now you're going to have to focus on making it though the next fifteen minutes."

She slowed, but didn't stop.

"Make that seconds." He cocked the gun.

Now she stopped.

"Hey, the light of reason! Drop the tongs and the gloves. Face the worktable. Don't make me ask twice." She obeyed, and a sense of control washed over his body.

Tears ran down her face.

"Hands behind your back; now bend over the table." He took out a roll of tape and bound her hands.

"Shamus, please, I can give you money."

"Do all you people go to victim school or something? Yesterday I wanted money. Thought that was clear by my tireless efforts to give you everything you asked for. Today, I just want to give you what you have coming."

"Please, what do you want?"

Better.

"Sit in this chair here so I can finish securing you." He taped her legs to the chair legs.

"There. Now, I have a gag if you get too vocal, but I have some questions." He strode over to her porcelain collection. "Myrtle, do you have any idea what it feels like to put all your effort and talent into something and then have all the hard work vanish? Through no fault of your own?"

She looked confused.

"Allow me to demonstrate." Shamus reached over to one of the custom shelves. "Here's a nice piece. I see you want eighteen hundred dollars; worth every penny, I'm sure." He lifted it one-handed and smashed the vase at her feet. "Whoops, all that hard work for nothing, huh?"

"Shamus, please. Take them and sell them. Take anything you want, but please don't hurt me."

"Take one, eh? There are so many to choose from. How about this one?" He selected another piece. "Nah, too boring." He flung the vase over his shoulder. Myrtle yelped when it shattered.

"How about a green one? No, that will clash with my rug." Crash. One by one, he broke every piece on display. Myrtle was quiet, but the tears rolled down her face. Shamus wished he had a plastic jar to collect the watery tribute to his power. Instead, he pretended to be moved.

"Oh, don't be like that, Myrtle. You can always make more, just like I can always make more sales. We're done. I need to gag you so I can leave." She didn't fight him, and he placed it in her mouth.

Porcelain shards littered the area. He picked up a long piece with cruel, sharp edges.

"There's just one more thing."

CHAPTER 42

Splitting Hairs

Newark, Delaware, Marlo Honda, Wednesday morning

Chang sat with Nelson in the cruiser. "We need to move fast. Soak up every impression."

"I'm not a Geiger counter. You can't just wave me in front of suspects until my eyes light up and you have your man." Nelson sounded irritated. Too bad. Chang would push Nelson and himself until Byrd stopped them or they caught the killer. He didn't want to frighten their quarry, either. Nelson couldn't scare a juvenile shoplifter, and sometimes people even relaxed around him.

Chang opened the car door. "Time to go to work."

* * *

The polished floors and gleaming cars reflected the banks of fluorescent lights in the ceiling.

A young man closed in on them. Male, Caucasian, medium height, brown hair. Not their man. "Good morning. Welcome to Marlo. I'm Scott. How may I help you gentlemen this morning?"

"We're here on business. May we see your manager?" Chang flashed his badge, and Scott disappeared.

A short, energetic man strode from a back door and looked them over.

"If you guys are from the Jehovah's Witnesses, you should know I'm a practicing Buddhist." He laughed enough for all three of them. Chang shook the offered hand and showed his credentials.

"Terry Cassidy, but everyone calls me 'Hop.' You know, short for Hopalong Cassidy." They walked to a glass-walled room, and he closed the door. "I assume you don't need a car, so what can I do for you?"

His smile looked puddle-deep.

"Did you have a customer here named Heather Cleary?" No big reaction.

"Any idea how many people we get through here? We're the region's volume leader."

"Congratulations. I'm sure you have a record of the sale. She came in last week and put a deposit on a car, and cancelled the deal."

"That happens. We don't like it, but that's life. Let me check the log." He swung a monitor around and typed in quick bursts. "Here it is. Yes, Heather Cleary cancelled her purchase of a gold V6 Accord last Friday. Stated reason: bought a BMW. Well, looks like we didn't lose that one over price. What do you want to know about her?"

Was he serious? "Do you read the papers or watch the news?"

"Mostly the sports pages. I need to stay upbeat. My ex-wife said I'm too focused."

Don't they all?

Chang tried to push away his dislike for the man and concentrate. "What do you know about the recent murders in the Wilmington area?"

"The serial killings? Weird, huh? What does it have to do with Heather Cleary?"

Chang stared at Hop's face and tried to read past the phony veneer.

"She was killed on Monday. Two days after she cancelled with your dealership." He watched Nelson out of the corner of his eye.

"Jesus! We don't like it when a customer cancels, but we don't send hit men after them."

Chang let the joke fall flat and watched the man squirm. "Can you tell me who the salesman was?"

"Do I have to?" Cassidy looked down at his book. "I'd rather you kept my people out of this. I can find out what you need to know."

"We have to talk to him ourselves. We could get a warrant, but your guy is one of a long list of people we need to see today. Are we going to find something we don't like?" Chang stood up and leaned over Cassidy. He put on his inscrutable expression.

"No…" Cassidy shied away from Chang until he reached the edge of his desk. "It's just that he's our best salesman, but we hired him even though he had some blemishes on his record. He doesn't like cops, and I don't want you to throw him off his game. He sells a lot of cars."

A lie. Chang could see from Nelson's body language that he didn't believe Cassidy's routine, either.

"What's his name, and is he in?"

"Walt Kerry, and yes, he's here. You can talk to him here, but try to keep it quiet. I don't need to remind you this is a business." He slipped out of his office.

"Told you it was a business. Some detective you are," Nelson said, looking up from his notes.

"What's he hiding?"

"Dunno. Something. You'll run checks on arrest records for both of them?"

"Sure, but I don't have time to waste on petty crimes." Chang assumed that almost everybody had some scam or another going. Motion caught his attention. "Look at this guy."

Walt Kerry, in his mid-twenties, had an enormous power-lifter's build. Larger than Chang's poker buddy, Carl Hull. Kerry wore an aggressive expression, but what made Chang's heart speed up was the closely cropped reddish hair.

CHAPTER 43
Whiff of Suspicion

Hop introduced Kerry to Chang and Nelson. Kerry said it was nice to meet them—his first lie. Cassidy left them alone in his office.

"What do you guys want with me?" Kerry looked at both of them. He did a double take when he saw Nelson.

Nelson used a nonchalant tone of voice. "We're doing routine follow-up; then we'll get out of your hair."

Chang got the hair reference.

"Follow-up of what? I haven't done anything. Ask Hop. I work here all the time."

Defensive right away. What disturbed Kerry's harmony?

"What can you tell me about Heather Cleary?"

"That bitch! We had a deal, and the stupid pothead backed out because she wanted a Beamer. She called me on Friday and wanted her damn deposit back. I should keep it. What's she saying now?"

Nelson jumped in before Chang could answer. "Not much. She's dead. Didn't you know?"

Chang tried to disguise his annoyance at the interruption.

"Huh? What did she do, wreck her new car? OD?"

Nelson said what Chang was thinking. "Does anyone around here read the papers?"

"Hop likes me to keep my mind clear. They're mostly bullshit, anyway. I worry about my own problems and my job, that's it. How'd she die?"

Chang took back control and watched Kerry's eyes dart around. "Murder, possibly connected to a series of killings in recent months. Does the name Midori ring a bell?"

"Rick Midori? Yeah, I sold him an Insight."

"Have you heard from him lately?"

"If he didn't have any problems with the car, then he's out of my life until he needs a new one. Wait, is he…?" Light dawned.

"With his ancestors, yes." Chang bore in. "What about the Hubberts, Patel, or Nguyens? Do you know them?"

"Whoa!" Kerry stood up like he'd been hit with a cattle prod. He glared at Chang. "I see what you're trying to do. You're after that serial killer guy, and you think I'm involved? You got the wrong guy, Charlie."

Charlie Chang. Cute. So the guy wasn't stupid.

"You *do* know about the killer." Chang overlooked the bluster. "I thought you didn't read the papers."

"I don't, but you'd have to be in a coma not to know something's going on. This is a small town… Hey! Are you sniffing me?" He stared at Nelson.

Nelson rocked away from Kerry. "No! Not exactly."

"Are you nuts?"

"Got a piece of paper says I'm not." Nelson stared at his notepad and began to scribble.

"Sit down, Kerry. We need your help to clear up a couple coincidences." Chang noticed Nelson had stopped watching. Why did he lose interest?

"I know my rights, and if I don't want to talk, you can't make me. I won't be railroaded into a jackpot." He sat and gripped the sides of the chair.

Perp slang. The guy must have a past.

"Would you rather waste our time all the way down at headquarters? Confucius say: If sale fall at Marlo, will it make sound in Dover?"

"Asshole. Fine, ask your fucking questions, then leave me alone."

"Okay, so you knew Heather and Rick Midori. What about the others? They all bought from here. What about the Hubberts?"

"Got a picture?"

Nelson pulled a folder out of a briefcase and slid the photo to Kerry.

"Aren't mine, but they look familiar. Big fatsos?"

"That's right." Chang ruled out a charm-school alibi.

"Ask around. It's easy to remember the ones who were pains in the ass. These guys look like they might have been." Kerry leaned back in his chair.

"What about Mr. Patel or the Nguyens?" Nelson asked. Kerry barked a laugh.

"We all have a *stack* of Patels. Nguyens, too. Let me guess, tough negotiators?" Kerry shook his head.

"I don't know," Nelson said.

"*I* do. You can show me a picture, but I doubt it would help; they all look…" Kerry looked at Chang and bit off his comment.

Same to you, round-eye. "We have everything we need. If there's anything else, we'll be in touch." Chang put out his hand, but Kerry ignored him.

"Next time you want to hassle me like that, I'll have a lawyer." Kerry's voice broke, and he wiped sweat off his lip. He opened the door and rushed out.

Chang took a few deep breaths and felt his blood pressure drop.

"That works?"

"Shu says it's good for me, but it's even better for the people who get under my skin."

Cassidy returned, and Chang got a copy of the salesmen's schedules from the last three months. On their way back to the car, Chang couldn't see Kerry but was sure he was watching them.

Chang waited until they were both in the car. "Who said you could take the lead during the interview?"

Nelson jumped at the harsh tone. "Needed him stirred up so I could read him. What's the paper for?"

Chang let it drop. "We can use the schedules to see who sold Marlo cars to the victims. Sounds like they won't all be by our friend." He pulled out of the parking lot.

Nelson leafed through the pages. "I wouldn't bother."

"I thought you weren't a Geiger counter." Chang could feel the first gray threads of a headache take root at the base of his skull.

"He's not a good person. He lies and he's got a mean streak. Scared too. It's all over him. But he's not our guy." Nelson returned to his scribbles.

"It all starts here. If not him, then who?" Chang knew better than to doubt Nelson's instincts, but his own said they were on the right trail.

Nelson smiled. "Kinda like porn at the Supreme Court—I'll know it when I see it. Who's next?"

CHAPTER 44
Mistaken Identity

Chang wanted to bolt out of the restaurant. An upscale pizza place was a good idea, but he regretted the choice at the first sight of ferns and brass rails.

Nelson got his usual vapor lock and ordered a plain cheese pie. Chang tried the pineapple and ham pizza at the breathless suggestion of the waiter. Guy knew his food despite the glitter makeup on his cheeks and frosted highlights on his bangs.

Outside Chang dug into his pocket for his car keys. He looked up when the door opened and the waiter walked toward them. Something in his hand. A flash of red… Chang reached for the pistol under his jacket.

The waiter pressed a silk ribbon into Nelson's palm and closed his fingers over it. He looked at Chang and spoke in a soft voice.

"I don't want to intrude. Just wanted to say how much my friends and I admire your courage to go out in public."

"Excuse me?" Chang said.

"Every day we're closer to a cure. Stay strong." The waiter winked at Nelson.

"Okay." Nelson stared at the AIDS awareness ribbon.

Chang's headache returned.

* * *

In the car, Chang rubbed his eyes and waited for the light to change.

"Why didn't you tell that waiter you weren't sick?"

Nelson looked surprised. "What for? It made his day."

"Never mind." Chang envied the waiter's sense of accomplishment. He and Nelson had little new to show for their efforts. The frustration worked its way into his hands and fused them to the steering wheel.

He picked up his notes from the arrest report they heard over the radio and waved them at Nelson. "We haven't ruled out Kerry. The timeline is feasible; his day off is Tuesday, and they're all off on Sundays. Lexus and BMW checked out, so unless the guy down the road at Patriot could have been at all the same places, we need to look hard at Kerry."

"But is a guy with a steroid bust and battery on his girlfriend *our* bad guy? Nope, though he may know more than he admits," Nelson said, putting the pages aside.

Chang turned into the parking lot for Patriot Motors. The large Honda logo sign towered above the sidewalk. A hugely overweight man rose from a desk positioned near the front door. Four hundred pounds, maybe more.

"Welcome to Patriot Motors, I'm Avery Fitz. Are you gentlemen here on business, or may I assist you with a new car?"

"What business would that be?"

"If you're not some sort of law enforcement, I'll have to turn in my salesman card." Avery looked over at Nelson.

"You I'm not sure about, but your friend… I'll bet a dinner I'm right. Believe me, that's a bet you don't want to lose." He patted his stomach and grinned.

"We need to speak to the manager." Chang didn't bother to take out his shield.

"That's Jake. Can I tell him what it's regarding?"

"Might be tough since you don't know."

Avery shrugged and walked back to get the manager.

They stood in the large glassed-in showroom. In his mind, Chang turned his impatience into a faceless blue figure he forced into a teak box with brass hinges.

Jake approached the men, introduced himself, and led them into his office.

"What's up, guys?"

"We're looking into a recent death. It could be foul play. She came through here, bought a car."

"Do you mean the girl killed on Monday?"

Chang nodded.

"Yeah, she did buy a car, but she was supposed to pick it up last week, I think last Friday. Never showed."

"Did she call to cancel?"

"I don't think she asked for her deposit back. You can see if the salesman caught up with her. I'll find out about a refund." Jake picked up the phone. "Nope, we never got a request." Jake paused.

Nelson leaned forward in his seat. "Who was the salesman?"

"Shamus Ryan, but he called in sick today."

"What day does Shamus normally have off?" Chang hoped to eliminate the guy.

Jake gestured to a printed schedule. "Tuesdays. He came in yesterday for a while, though. Why?"

Tuesdays? "Can I get a copy of that?" Chang pointed at the schedule. He tried to appear the bored cop he was a moment ago. His instincts twitched, colors in the room grew sharper.

"Take this one." Jake handed it to Chang.

Chang's cell phone rang, and he excused himself and took the call. His ears roared with blood when he returned. "We have to cut this short. Mr. Barlow, thanks for your time, and we'll be back to speak to your salesman."

* * *

"I'll fill you in while we roll." Chang backed up the car and chirped the tires. "The killer's on a sprint." Chang hit the emergency lights without the siren and wove through traffic toward downtown and the on-ramp for 95 South.

"Where are we going?"

"Newark. I want to beat the press there. They're going to have a field day with this one." Chang whipped the car around a dump truck and punched the accelerator. He entered the ramp and was doing over eighty by the time he merged.

"Well?" Nelson gripped the armrest.

"We're going to a development called Carpenter Woods. A little while ago a neighbor noticed that the basement window at the house next to hers was totally smashed. She called it in, and guess what the county police found?"

"The owner."

"You're partially right."

"Meaning?"

"They found *most* of the owner."

CHAPTER 45
On the Ball

Chang stopped around the corner from the crime scene in Carpenter Woods. "Walk around back and I'll sneak you in."

"We break the chain of evidence if I go in unregistered." Nelson stared at him and didn't move.

"We'll ask for forgiveness later."

"What if we screw up the case?"

"You see what the guy's doing. You really think it will come down to lab results?" Chang didn't care what happened afterward. This one wasn't going to slip away because of paperwork.

Nelson's face scrunched up. His own internal debate, probably. His expression cleared, and he gave Chang a little smile.

"I was bored with computers anyhow."

Chang had never heard Nelson admit that before.

"Go to the back. I'll wave you in."

Chang drove up to the tape, and the officer allowed him to enter. The police concentrated their barricade efforts on the main road. Maybe Nelson could climb over a couple fences.

Chang signed in, put on his paper suit, and went in the front door.

Inside, he saw rage's hangover. It looked like someone had taken a huge red roller and redecorated the house with savage feng shui. His emotions caught up a moment later. All blood.

The evidence flags on the blood spots were so redundant that he choked back a bitter laugh. Need more sleep.

Chang went to the back door and looked out. He saw movement in the bushes, and Nelson's scratched-up face popped out like a crazy flower. One uniformed officer stood nearby and turned at the sound.

Chang opened the back door and shouted to the officer.

"Keep this yard clear! There's press coming in, and I don't want any of them to sneak around the side." Chang pointed. The uniform moved close to the window where the killer had broken in. Chang heard rustling, but Nelson was out of sight.

"The last thing we need is to let some clever photographer sneak in through the window. I wouldn't mind seeing them get cut, but we can't have more blood down there. I'll lock the back door."

The overall chaos out front helped. Chang returned inside and saw Nelson crouching below the windows.

"Are you okay?"

"Thorns." Nelson wiped blood off his face. "I'm fine."

They went down the hall, and Chang noticed the hall closet ajar. He peeked inside with a penlight.

"He hid in there." The closet faced the living room. Smears of blood led into the hall. He stepped into the living room. The scuff marks and spray of blood on the wall told him where the victim went down, but not out.

The rest of the hallway revealed a far more intense struggle.

"Brave boy, you clobbered him from behind." Nelson looked around while he spoke.

Chang saw from the pictures in the room that Mr. Stiles was a big man. The rug in the living room bunched up in one place and told him the killer had dragged the body instead of carrying it. He followed the marks to the second-floor stairs.

"Got tired? Heavier than you thought. Going for the tub?" Nelson asked the empty house. The sticky pool on the floor showed where the killer had dragged the body to the basement.

They both jumped at the rattle of the front doorknob.

"Get downstairs; I'll buy us a couple minutes," Chang said.

* * *

Chang picked up the coppery scent even before he got to the mess in the basement.

Nelson was standing over the body. "What happened?"

"Rookie tech wanted a look, forgot to check if I was done. I bit her head off. I'll apologize later." Chang winced at the inadvertent choice of words.

He did his best to block out the horror of the headless corpse face down, if there had been a face. A large amount of blood puddled near the neck. Bits of tissue on the bow saw next to the body left little doubt about the method of decapitation. Chang saw the other wood saws on the wall.

Another improvisation, like at the Hubberts'. He felt Nelson stare at him.

"What?"

Nelson pointed down with his finger. "It's personal."

Chang shifted his attention to the stump.

A crimson-soaked tennis ball was lodged in the base of the severed neck. Chang checked his gloves and tugged at the soggy felt. His fingers slipped, and then the ball came free with a wet sucking sound. He held the ball up and saw a silvery painted smiley face with "Have a nice day" scrawled on the side.

"See the fancy ink? Wanted to make sure you could see it."

"Stands out well from the blood." Chang took a deep breath. The ball felt heavy and cold in his hand. He put it back near the stump.

"Why that now?" Nelson began to rock.

Chang refused to allow the kaleidoscope of images to disrupt his train of thought. Dead faces from the near and distant past jockeyed for his attention, and his trash can swirled in the mix. Out of instinct he tried to put the faces in the can. Topper first... The sharp pain in his temple told him the can belonged with the images. It wasn't another teak box. He saw his mangled bonsai tree. The trash picker?

Chang felt scales rub the bars of its cage. The killer was stalking him? "Come on, then!" The Dragon's voice filled the basement. Chang tried to conjure the sneak's masked face. He reached for the tennis ball to burst it in his fist. Red curtains shrouded his vision.

"Evidence." Nelson's voice arrowed into his mind, and Chang stopped. He saw Nelson had backed away from him.

"Flannigan might have told the killer things about me. He didn't pull any punches. Some guy went through my trash…" Chang took three deep breaths. The Dragon curled up again.

Chang looked back to the body for any other personal statements, and a patch of blood patterns on the floor brought him back to his task. The dime-sized droplets of blood a few feet from the body made no sense at first. Then he understood.

"He held the head up here to drain. See how the blood fell a few feet? Is he into trophies now?" Chang turned to Nelson.

Nelson looked more pale than usual. "Welcome back. Was that…"

"Never mind." Chang heard the hitch in his voice and fought for control.

Nelson looked at him. "I've seen enough. You better get me out of here. We can't afford to get thrown off the case now."

CHAPTER 46

Details, Details

Patriot Motors, Thursday evening

Shamus drummed his fingers on his desk. Ever since he'd learned the police wanted to speak with him, he couldn't focus. Jake said they were tying up some loose ends around the death of Heather Cleary.

"One of them wasn't even a real cop, I don't think. Did Heather ever call you to cancel the deal? We don't have a request form for the refund of her deposit."

"I haven't heard a peep from her since before last Friday. I called her house a thousand times to find out where she was. Poor kid. I wonder what she was mixed up in." Shamus shook his head.

"Yeah. Well, they might be back in the morning, so try not to schedule any appointments if you can help it. But we need to pick it up this month, so do what you have to do." Jake sounded bored with the topic. Good.

"I doubt I'll be much help. Hey, maybe they want a car!" Shamus faked a smile.

"Might get rid of them quicker." Jake walked away.

Dammit, I told you, Gran! Shamus knew he should have left that spoiled worm alone. His mouth felt dry at the idea that they'd linked Heather to him. A smart cop might start to see other connections, and that could lead to problems.

Shamus pretended to listen to Hank rant about some customer who came in last week and wasted his time, as if that didn't happen to all of them.

Then something about what Hank had just said broke into his train of thought. Shamus felt the tingle of an idea.

CHAPTER 47

Miles to Go

Newark, early Friday morning

Colleen used to call Chang's occupational insomnia "case-lag." Since he'd left Nelson's, his mind had been racing and he hadn't been able to calm his thoughts despite his best efforts. He needed sleep, but wouldn't get it. He lived in interesting times.

When he'd checked his answering machine earlier, he was still on the case. Bad news, one of the officers at the Stiles crime scene had spotted Nelson when he left the house. It was his friend D'Agostino, and he let Chang know that his secret was safe. It wouldn't last. The security would tighten at each scene. But Chang knew they'd break the case if Byrd didn't break them first. Chang felt like an ant in the bottom of an hourglass. The sand pressed down…

Shu opened the door. Chang didn't bother to scold him for not checking who it was.

"She is asleep." Shu stepped aside.

His mother was a reliable night owl. She must have had a difficult day. Shu read the question in his eyes.

"Pain better now."

"You should have called me."

"It passed."

"Shu, it's not indigestion." She never tired of complaining that the colon surgery from several years back only spread her cancer, despite tests to the contrary. She did have painful flare-ups, not that it stopped her from enjoying Shu's cooking.

Some days the pain made her an old woman; others she looked like she would live forever.

"Always eye out for one trouble too many. Come downstairs, Master Paul."

Chang followed.

* * *

Soon he was bathed in sweat on the bare wood floor. His aching muscles protested the stretches. He held still and forced his mind to clear. Shu ran him through the mental purification steps.

"What see now?" Shu stood behind Chang and carried his bamboo stick.

Chang kept his eyes closed. In his mind he paddled across a lake, floated across the snowy plain, and climbed up a barren mountain. "I'm near the top." He jumped at the sting from Shu's stick.

"Start over."

"But—"

"If hear *me*, not lost in moment. Again."

He looked at the clock and saw it was after two o'clock in the morning Shu's stick scolded.

Chang returned to the lake and began to paddle.

CHAPTER 48

Gone in a Blink

Chang reached home before dawn. He saw the message light blinking on his answering machine. His cell never rang, so it must not have been an emergency, but he crossed the room and hit the button before he hung up his keys.

"Paul, it's Colleen. Sorry to call so early, or is it late?"

What kept her awake at night?

"Guess who I saw, in the creaky flesh, this afternoon in the editor's office? Handshakes and everything. You may not have to worry about Flannigan kicking you around much more. That's good news, right? I'll keep you posted..."

She paused, and Chang could picture her chewing her knuckle until she could find her cigarettes.

"I read his pieces. Scary. You got a bad guy down there. Be careful, huh?"

* * *

Gone. Chang stared at the ceiling. Why couldn't Colleen have been at her mother's house when the Nightmare came? Anywhere but next to him.

He didn't need to be asleep to see the Tong, poised over his bed with the moonlight's glint on the edge of the blade.

He still didn't know whether to thank or curse his reflexes. He failed to block the knife slash on his neck, but he reacted fast enough to keep his arteries from pumping his life onto the sheets.

He could smell the spice on the assassin's black shirt and see the eyes filled with manic purpose. The killer never got another chance to fulfill his contract. The Dragon snapped awake, and Chang held the attacker's wrist with one hand and used his other fist to batter the man's windpipe.

Chang watched the man die struggling for air that had no way to reach his lungs. He looked like a fish, his mouth opening and closing soundlessly. Chang held the phone with one hand and a blood-soaked pillow against his bleeding neck. He made sure the man was dead before he called the ambulance, but he passed out before they arrived. The first Nightmare came in the hospital. No Colleen to worry about back then, only the tubes he pulled out before he woke up, and the killer he'd fought disappearing with the mists of his dream.

For years the Nightmare stayed buried. After they moved to Delaware, Chang thought maybe it was gone forever. He never knew why it eventually returned, but he doubted a psychiatrist would have shed any light.

What he did know was that the Nightmare *did* return, and he'd woken up to find his fingers wrapped around Colleen's throat. He let go instantly, but she never shared a bed with him again. She couldn't understand why he didn't believe in Western psychoanalysis, but she was just as stubborn about giving Shu's training a chance.

After each shooting in New York, he was required to see a department psychiatrist. Worthless. Colleen refused to entertain the possibility that an ancient culture might yield a better approach.

Soon it didn't matter who was right. The guest bedroom wasn't far enough. A couple months after the Nightmare, she was gone.

CHAPTER 49

Click Click Click

Wilmington, Delaware, Friday morning

Chang felt a sense of déjà vu. He and Nelson sat in the car near Patriot Motors and waited. Shamus Ryan was due in for the early shift.

Nelson looked haggard. Chang hadn't slept either, but his mind was clear.

Still no sign of Larry Stiles's head. The media had pounced on the story, and a tasteless cartoon appeared in the press that showed a severed head and a talk balloon that said, "Could be worse. I know where the cops' heads are!"

The retraction and apology carried an attorney's warmth.

Chang learned from neighbors that Larry lived alone, had few friends, and led a quiet life. He asked whether Larry had recently purchased a new car, possibly a Honda?

No, he owned a red Dodge pickup only a year or two old. One neighbor said he kept it immaculate.

How Stiles fit in was still a mystery. The cops combed the house without success. Nelson was sure the killer had taken the head. The media obtained a picture of Stiles for the evening news, but unlike the stupid cartoon, the photo might bring out a witness. For now, the killer was accelerating faster than they could pick up clues.

Chang and Nelson compared the timeline of the killings and the work schedules of Walt Kerry from Marlo and this guy Shamus from Patriot. Both were off on Tuesdays, and the dealerships were closed on Sundays.

Heather Cleary was killed sometime in the morning last Monday. Phone records showed a call came in to her cell from the pay phone at the nearby gas station around nine thirty in the morning. Walt Kerry was scheduled to be at work that morning, though Shamus wasn't.

After they talked with Shamus, Chang was going to give the manager at Marlo a call to confirm that Kerry was actually at work that day. He'd also catch up with the salesman who'd worked with the Hubberts.

Chang checked his watch again and tried to remain calm. Nelson would pick up on his anxiety. "Are you *sure* you want to go in alone?"

"I need to read this guy. You'd scare him and jam me." Nelson picked up his notebook. "Besides, it'll be in a public place. What's he going to do?"

"Shoot you? Stab you? Cut your head off?" Chang tamped down his frustration.

"It's *my* plan." Nelson opened the car door. "You have the number for my new cell phone?"

"On my speed dial." Chang felt a drop of sweat crawl down his ribcage.

* * *

Shamus sat in the break room and pretended to read the newspaper. Ideas ricocheted around his mind until Jake came in.

"Famous Shamus, one of the guys from yesterday is here to see you."

Nice of him not to say police, but it wouldn't take long for word to get around. He followed Jake to his office.

Was this a joke? He saw a middle-aged scarecrow with black hair on top of a hungry face. The dark eyes glittered, only spark about the guy.

"Shamus Ryan, this is Nelson Rogers, with the state police." Jake left after they shook hands. His fingers felt like eels.

"Nice to meet you, Mr. Ryan, and I'm not exactly 'with' the police. More like the world's oldest intern."

"Call me Shamus." Big smile.

"Very good. And make it Nelson, please. I get enough Mr. Rogers jokes as it is." Fake laugh. The guy acted nervous, but the eyes seemed to drill into Shamus.

"Sorry to have missed you yesterday." That name sounded familiar.

"The officer I'm assigned to help out was called away. Maybe you saw the reason all over the news."

Where are you going with that, Mr. Not-a-cop? "Yes, terrible. Are you any closer to catching someone?" Shamus's voice was smooth, but his heart rate picked up.

"They don't tell me much. I'm just helping chase down pesky details."

"Is that what I am? A pesky detail?" Shamus saw the guy begin to sweat. Better.

Shamus wasn't fooled. If anyone heard more lies than a cop, it was a car salesman. Nelson knew more.

"That came out wrong, didn't it? My partner talks to the critical witnesses. So in this case, it's good to be less important." Nelson gave another nervous laugh. "We noticed that Heather Cleary put down deposits on several cars.

We thought maybe she said or did something that might be useful."

"Be glad they sent over the junior varsity, eh?" Shamus felt control seep back into his bones. "Never did hear back after she missed her delivery. Jake already told you she didn't put in a request for a refund?"

"Yes. Thanks for answering my first question." The guy fumbled through some notes. "Sorry. I'm so out of practice I can barely make it through a simple interview."

Shamus chuckled. "You should have seen me with my first customer. I was more scared of them than they were of me." You tipped your hand, "intern." Out of practice means you used to do this. Once a cop, always a cop.

"Here we are. Did she seem upset or afraid to you?"

Shamus pictured Heather's face when he opened the car door. Don't laugh. Not here.

"No. I think she just wanted to get the sale over with and leave is all. Was there anything else?" Before you sweat through your shirt?

Nelson inhaled deeply through his nose. Weird.

"No, but if you think of anything unusual Heather said or did, please call me." Nelson handed him a card that read "Technology Consultant" and bore the state police logo. What a piece of work.

"Sorry I wasn't more help. It's awful what happened to her." Shamus stood.

"Were you as mad as some of the other salesman when she cancelled?"

X-ray eyes swept through him again. Shamus suppressed a shudder.

"Well, she never called me to cancel, so I wondered what happened that night. Once she was in the news, I really wasn't too worried about losing a sale." Nice try.

"I guess not. Stupid question. Don't mind me, I'm older than I look." Nelson's cell phone began to ring.

Shamus smiled. "Saved by the bell. If we're done, I'll let you take your call." Nelson nodded and shook Shamus's hand.

This time, despite the weak grip, Shamus felt like he was grabbing a joy buzzer. Mind trick. Stay frosty. You're the Ice-man!

Shamus stepped out of the office and strolled back to his desk. We're not done by a long shot, cop.

CHAPTER 50
Shards

Chang hung up and drove in front of the showroom. He glanced through the large window into the sales desk area.

Hard eyes snatched his attention. A red-haired man with a boyish face stared through the window directly at Chang. Shamus Ryan.

Chang thought he saw a smile and then realized the guy was baring his teeth. The hair on his neck tingled, and he suppressed an urge to burst out of the car. He barely noticed Nelson approach the car. When he looked back, Ryan was gone.

Nelson yanked the door open and hopped in.

"How'd it go?" Chang pulled out onto Pennsylvania Avenue.

"Smelled like just before a thunderstorm. Ozone, electric…"

"Stay with me. What did he say?" Nelson's anxiety was contagious.

"Say? He was polite and charming. We had a lovely chat…and I think I was going to sweat blood if I stayed any longer."

In his mind, Chang could see victims swirl around the image of the fresh-faced salesman. Eyes and teeth… He noticed a tremor in Nelson's hand. "How did he react to you?"

"Hope he thinks I'm an idiot, but I don't know. He throws off so many signals. Like spinning the dial on a radio…fear, anger, lust, hate." Nelson found a near-empty water bottle on the car floor and shook the last few drops into his mouth. "What happened while I was gone?"

"A woman called in a tip that panned out about thirty minutes ago. They found the head."

Nelson closed his eyes. "Details."

"The lady saw the piece on the news last night about Stiles and recognized him. Her friend, an artist from up in Arden, was pals with Stiles, and when she saw the report, she tried to reach her. She left messages, but finally got nervous and called the cops." Chang paused to let Nelson absorb the information.

"What did they find?"

"Victim in her studio, strapped to a chair, throat cut. They think done with a broken piece of her pottery."

"The head?"

"It was on display, dunked in glaze and kiln-fired. One cop puked, but otherwise they kept the scene intact." Chang didn't think he could give Nelson a firsthand look and told him so. Did it matter?

* * *

They reached Arden a few minutes later, and Chang found the winding driveway to the Maynard house.

"Don't see any new cars." Nelson peeked out from his hiding place under a blanket in the back seat.

"I forgot to tell you. The county cop said the tipster recognized Stiles because the victim bragged that he was helping her get a great deal on a new minivan."

"A Honda?" Nelson's voice sounded muffled.

"I'd put money on it. We shouldn't stay here long. We'll have plenty to connect the dots to this guy Shamus once we look."

"Wish I hadn't talked to him now. Think we can get a tail on him?"

Chang stopped the car and spun around to address the lump on the back-seat floor. "Forget backup right now. Byrd won't buy it, and then we might risk losing him for good. I don't trust anybody down there."

Silence. The victims came in so fast. The memories layered on him, and Chang could smell the victims even when he was awake. His anger swelled in a thick red tide.

He left Nelson hidden in the car and entered the crime scene after he'd sleepwalked through the procedural formalities.

Chang opened the side entrance to a garage door. The smell of burned flesh still clung to the air. Sunlight filled the studio, and he saw the back of a woman's head, tipped forward and lifeless. The white hair made Chang wonder what wisdom had died with her. No respect for age…

He walked closer and saw an elaborate set of display shelves, empty save for the grisly sculpture that faced the woman. The misshapen sockets seemed to accuse him.

"I've been too slow." He remembered the happy man in the photos at the Stiles home.

Pottery fragments lay heaped at the feet of the female victim. A long, knifelike shard covered in blood was balanced on top of the pile. Chang was careful to avoid the rest of the blood on the floor. Silvery tape bound the victim's arms. No tennis balls in sight.

He walked outside and wondered how many minutes they had before the next wave of press. The coverage grew by the day. And why not? They had fresh meat on a regular basis. He tore off his paper suit.

* * *

"Bad as it sounded?" Nelson still hid under the blanket in the back seat.

The snowy fields Chang conjured had turned blood-red. The mountains, piles of pottery shards.

"Worse." Chang closed the car door. "This has to stop. If we don't find what we need, let's get him anyway. If he fights…" Chang didn't finish the sentence.

Nelson's phone beeped, and for a moment Chang was puzzled because he was the only one who called it. Then he remembered they'd programmed it to signal when Nelson's office voice mail had a message. His suspension didn't affect his phone.

Nelson punched in the number and pass code. He blanched and handed the cell to Chang.

"Mr. Rog…uh, Nelson. Shamus Ryan here. You asked me to call you if I remembered anything. I was home for lunch and saw a news report about the killings. They showed pictures of the victims, and I recognized a couple of them. They were in my dealership and talked to our assistant manager, Hank Grant. Could I meet you at your office today around five o'clock? Don't want Hank to see me talking to you again. I'll leave early. Call me back at my home number if you can meet me." He left the number and ended the message.

"What do you make of that?" Chang asked.

Nelson took the phone. "A string of lies."

"Sure. But do you think he's trying to throw us off the trail or put us onto this guy, Hank?"

"Maybe both. Call him back and tell him you'll be glad to talk to him. I'll set up a wire for the interview room in case he says anything really stupid." Chang's blood pounded into his muscles in anticipation of a chase.

"Can you get warrants for the tap, and his place?"

"Eventually. His address is in there." Chang pointed to a folder.

"Byrd's going to know I'm involved." Nelson didn't sound worried, just matter-of-fact.

"Yes." If Byrd stopped them now, Chang would make sure he'd take the mistake to an early grave.

CHAPTER 51

Too Close for Comfort

Greenville, Delaware, Friday afternoon

Sometimes he scared himself. Shamus hung up his phone and looked at the clock. Quarter to one and time to get back to the dealership. Just a few details to wrap up.

Earlier that morning, his head was pounding so hard he thought his nose would gush blood again. His conversation with that nervous semi-cop gnawed at him. The dork knew something. How much?

It wasn't the questions Nelson asked him, but the ones he didn't ask. With all the killings, why no mention of any others? If one victim had a connection, wouldn't they check if maybe some others might? Shamus figured he could play off the links to customers who didn't buy, but he expected the topic to come up. When it didn't, it spooked him.

Soon the cops would discover Myrtle's final resting place as an "objet d'art." If they asked about her at the dealership, he knew the other salesman would remember "Shamus's girlfriend." That wouldn't do.

He considered some kills out of state, to throw off the cops. Then it hit him why he recognized Nelson's name. His research! He'd shredded the pages on Chang and his screw-ups in New York, but he could swear Nelson Rogers was the name of his old partner. The guy had gone crazy or something, but it looked like he'd gotten better. Shamus realized everything might collapse before he got a chance to escape.

The walls of his apartment closed in, and he turned up the stereo to mask his screams of frustration. This time, the panic didn't subside. It fed on his voice, and he imagined his head was going to burst into flames. He ran to the bathroom, no time to fill the sink, and jammed his head into the toilet bowl.

Fear gave way to clarity. Lots of men did their best thinking in there, didn't they?

His hair dripped, and he flushed the toilet out of reflex. His laughter bounced off the tiles.

Maybe he *should* leave town, but he needed a little more time.

Was Nelson the only guy who could pull it all together? Nobody had scared him like that before. Made him humiliate himself like that…

Shamus wanted to finish on his own terms. He had twenty grand from Myrtle that would help him go underground fast, but not before he pried some answers from that nosy scarecrow.

Nelson wasn't a prospective customer, so Shamus didn't know where he lived. The guy worked at state police headquarters, but that was a little too bold. He would have tailed him back to his home, but he didn't have that kind of time.

On a hunch, he opened up the phone book to the white pages and checked the name on the card. Right after Rogers, Nancy, there it was: Rogers, Nelson. Not "N" Rogers, but

Nelson. The address was in Bear, probably in those apartments or town houses. Not a hunch. Destiny. Game on!

* * *

Earlier Shamus had taken off around eleven thirty for "lunch" and picked up some supplies on the way home. Now, with his call made to the police, all he needed was to confirm that they'd taken the bait and he would move forward. If they didn't call back, plan B was to skip town and seek his future straightaway.

He had everything staged by his front door. He'd packed light and left most of his possessions in place. He made sure the gas cans were tightly sealed and that all the cash was in a canvas bag with some clothes. He tucked the revolver in a holster in the small of his back. It would be uncomfortable, especially when he drove, but his jacket would keep it covered during his shift.

He shook Gran's picture again and then panned the front hallway to show her his work.

"All your fault, you know. Had to make me take the dirty girl, didn't you? Now I've got to clean up *your* mess." She sent no message, because she knew he was right.

He picked up the antique cowbell. Funny, he didn't remember when he'd bought it, just noticed it one day.

"Fair's fair. Time for your punishment." He did his best to match the slow, deliberate clang she always used.

He returned the picture to the freezer and took the turquoise and brass urn with her ashes. He added hot water from the kitchen tap and swirled.

Shamus poured the sludgy mixture into his ice-cube trays and returned them to the freezer. Tiny curls of steam looked like smoke.

Finally, he took down the now vast collection of articles and fed them to his garbage disposal.

* * *

At the dealership, Shamus took the parking space behind Hank's car and popped the hood. He checked the oil for show and yanked a fuse, which he put in his pocket. He checked his messages at home. Nelson had fallen for it. No turning back now.

CHAPTER 52
Ties That Bind

Both Shamus and Hank were scheduled to leave at five o'clock. He slipped out before Hank.

In his car, Shamus cranked the engine, which didn't start. Hank approached, and Shamus got out in disgust. He opened the hood and cursed.

"What's wrong?" Hank peered into the engine bay.

"Damn! I know exactly what it is. One of the clips for my fuses came loose. Happened before. The fuse drops out, and then the car won't start. That's just great!"

"Can you find it?"

"It must have fallen out on the way. I have a spare at home. Crap!"

Hank looked amused at Shamus's misfortune. "Can't you get another from service?"

"They're out, thanks to me."

"Sounds like you need a new car, man. Can I interest you in a Honda?" Hank laughed.

"Maybe. But first I need to get home. Can I ask you a huge favor, Hank?"

He could tell Hank thought he knew what was next. "I have to go, man. Dot is meeting me at the mall…"

"Please, I have a date later, and well, I don't get many of those, so I can't be late. I live close by. Tell you what, I'll hook you up with not one, but two lunches from Sugarloafs. One for each way. What do you say?"

"Must be some girl. All right, let's make it quick." They climbed into Hank's late-model Accord demo. "See how it starts right up?" Hank grinned.

When they reached the apartment, Shamus looked over at Hank.

"While you're here, can you come up real quick and tell me which tie I should wear tonight? I know it's stupid, but if anyone knows ties, it's you. I'll grab the fuse while you look. Won't take a sec."

"Why not?"

Hank was all smiles now that he was properly bribed. Shamus unlocked his front door and pointed toward his bedroom.

"The ties are in there on the bed; I'll get that fuse."

Hank took a few steps into the apartment and stopped. "You really live here?" He sniffed and looked over at the gas cans.

"Hey man, that's not safe. Why do you have gas indoors?" Hank jumped at the sound of the slammed door.

"Alone at last." Shamus held his revolver.

"Is this some sort of joke? Don't point that at me; I don't care if it isn't loaded. I learned in the navy, never point a weapon unless you're going to use it."

Shamus needed to move him down the learning curve a little quicker.

"It *is* loaded. Shut up and do what you're told."

"I'm out of here, man." Hank sounded frightened and stopped cold when Shamus aimed the gun at his head.

"Crash course, Hank. Stick with me. Lots of people getting dead in Wilmington. Two things in common. They all deserved it, and they all shopped at Patriot. Cops came yesterday and again this morning. They only want to talk to one person. Is this coming together for you yet?"

Hank was smarter than he acted. Shamus could see the wheels working. He turned pale, an excellent sign.

"My God," he whispered.

"There's my man! You can see me in a whole new light, can't you? Take your time, I don't show off my radiance to everyone." It felt good to share.

"Why me? Why would you want to hurt me?"

Shamus needed Hank under control for the next part to go smoothly.

"I've got good news. Listen carefully. Actually, sit down. You don't look so good." Shamus gestured toward a chair. Hank sat.

"I need you, and when I'm done I have no interest in hurting you. Do what I say and don't try anything stupid, and we're both going to be fine. Desperate people try stuff. Make sense so far?"

Hank just stared.

"C'mon, buddy, I need a little feedback here."

"What do I do?"

"I'll get to that. We have a short drive ahead. Going to see a friend. Don't get any crazy ideas. Police will have a big interest in me soon, so you're an insurance policy. I need a head start. The gas is going with us so I can get farther without stopping in public."

"Why me?"

"Oh, hey, don't take it personally; you just happened to come out to the car." The lie felt smooth on his tongue.

"Where will you go?"

"I could tell you, but then I'd have to kill you." Shamus laughed hard. "I've always wanted to say that!" He turned serious. "Okay, time to get to work. Put on those coveralls and hat." Shamus pointed to the items on a wall hanger.

Hank nodded. He looked like he might faint. Shamus needed him alert.

"Snap out of it, soldier! You're going to drive us down to Bear. Once you finish dressing, grab the gas cans." Shamus donned his own coveralls and cap. Now they were two painters. He shouldered his backpack and picked up the money bag. He kept the revolver out of sight in his other hand.

After they loaded everything into Hank's car, Shamus ordered him into the driver's seat and sat behind him.

Shamus gave directions and said nothing further. Hank was wobbly at first but seemed to regain his composure. By all indications he was clinging to the hope that he would survive if he followed instructions. People could be so funny!

Near the apartment complex they waited at a light and a state police cruiser pulled up next to them. Shamus held the pistol out of sight and with his other hand gave a little wave. The bored-looking cop nodded and returned his gaze to the road.

Shamus saw Hank's hands tighten on the wheel. His breathing sped up, and sweat stains bloomed on the painter's cap. Hank inched the car forward and stopped, then did it again.

"I know you aren't that stupid. You're dead before the cop can say 'license and registration'."

Shamus promised himself he'd put Hank through agony before the cop got him. How fucking long was this light, anyway? He felt smothered in the painter outfit.

The light turned green. Hank let out a little squeak, but the car accelerated at a normal pace. The trooper pulled ahead, and both of them let out a breath when he turned down another road.

At quarter to six they pulled into the development of town houses and apartments. There was a large parking lot for the apartments. Town houses had spots in front. Shamus saw the street for Nelson's house and told Hank to park in the big lot, where the car would blend in.

He left the bag and the gas cans in the trunk and took the backpack. Shamus could see commuters arriving. He loved the painter outfits. He could just stomp all over the place and people wouldn't give it a second thought. He and Hank found the house and walked around to the back. A couple neighbors several lots away waved. Sheep!

They walked up the stairs to the back door, and Shamus handed Hank a small crowbar to pry it open.

Hank gripped the bar, and his knuckles turned white.

"Bad idea. The pistol's cocked. It's a hair trigger."

Hank gasped when a dog howled and thumped against the door. Shamus thought quickly.

"The dog's harmless, just barks. Open the door; I'm right behind you." Shamus hoped he'd get a chance to see the dog attack Hank. Too funny.

Hank opened the door but hesitated. The barks increased. Shamus still couldn't see how big it was. He snatched the crowbar and shoved Hank in.

Hank squawked and fell to the floor. Shamus came in behind him. He closed the door but stayed ready in case he needed to escape from an attack dog. He looked over and saw that the "attack dog" had stopped barking and was sniffing the prone Hank. A basset hound. Wary, but not vicious. Shamus hid his disappointment.

"See? I told you. Trust me, Hank. Stick to the plan and you'll be okay."

Shamus didn't need any wild cards when the dog's master came home, and he didn't want to scare Hank. Not yet.

"Hank, put the dog in the closet by the front door. I'll be watching, so don't keep going out the front."

Shamus applauded when Hank finished. The dog scratched at the door, but otherwise caused no trouble. Shamus checked his watch. Quarter past six. Not much time.

"Okay, Hank, after my friend tells me what I need to know, I'll leave. Until then, sit in this chair and I'll tie you up..."

Hank must have read the details on some of the cases.

"You're gonna kill me, aren't you?" Hank panted like Nelson's dog. His eyes opened wide, and his head swiveled around. Searching for a weapon? Escape? Shamus began to feel lightheaded and realized he was breathing just as fast. He'll screw it up!

"Calm down, Hank."

"I don't wanna die, I don't wanna die."

Hank didn't even hear him. His feet were shoulder-width apart. Hank would run soon...

Shamus pointed his foot and kicked Hank in the groin. Hank curled up on the floor with a new focus.

"I know just how you feel. Got a soccer ball there once. Get up. Sit in the chair."

Hank struggled into the seat. Fifty-fifty that he'd puke.

"You made me nervous. I'll stay back here. Don't get up."

Hank nodded.

"Stay put and let me pace the floor in peace." Shamus pulled out a blackjack and wrapped a small towel around it to prevent a scalp wound. No sense making a bloody mess. He walked back and forth a couple of times, and when Hank began to relax, he swung the lead-filled weapon into the back of his head.

Hank gave a grunt and fell to the floor. Out cold. Cool! Shamus hog-tied him with plenty of tape and gagged him in case he woke up anytime soon. Much better. No animals on the loose.

CHAPTER 53

Uninvited

Dover, Friday

By ten after six, Chang knew Shamus wouldn't show up.

Chang stood. "I bet he's on the run. Do you think we might find him at home?"

"Probably not."

"It's worth a try. Ready?" Chang moved toward the stairs.

They jumped into the car, and Chang sped up Route 1.

Chang grabbed his cell to check on the status of the search warrant for Shamus's place. Nothing yet.

"Try his house again. If you reach him, keep him on the line as long as possible." Chang didn't hold much hope. Nelson dialed and got the machine again.

When traffic permitted, Chang kept the car over ninety. Dotted lines on the road flicked past. Screw the warrant.

When they were close to Bear, Chang hit the brakes and took the exit to Nelson's.

"What are you doing?"

"We need answers. I can get in and out of his place without anyone knowing I was there. I could be prosecuted if anyone sees me, including you."

"I'd never tell on you!"

"You stink at lying." No time to worry about Nelson's feelings. "Go walk Daisy. You never know what I might do."

"Huh?"

"Say I'm out for a drive and I find myself at a certain apartment, to ask directions. If the door swung open and I observed incriminating evidence, we could wait for a warrant. If he's home, it's not my fault I if I have to protect myself."

"What if he protects himself first?"

"Get out of the car. I don't think I'm going to find him, anyway."

Nelson sounded resigned. "I guess I'm not much help if he's home." He got out of the car.

"Keep that phone with you." Chang hit the gas.

* * *

Shamus heard footsteps and the jingle of keys in the lock. His heart sped up, and the dog barked. Shamus crept toward the door, pistol in hand. He saw Nelson walk in, but his head turned toward the noisy closet.

"Daisy? How did you…"

Shamus walked forward, and Nelson pivoted and froze in place.

"Sorry I missed our meeting. Over here, no noise. Hands up, against the wall." Nelson complied. Even more docile than Midori. Shamus grabbed one arm and shoved him. Nelson faced it. Shamus patted him down, but he only found a cell phone, no gun. Good. He put the cell on the dining room table.

"I didn't think you carried. You're not exactly Dirty Harry, are you?"

"I'm an intern, remember?"

Shamus laughed and grabbed his wrists. "That's pretty good." This goober was skinny! Shamus felt braver. He used some tape to bind Scarecrow's hands behind his back.

"How'd you find me?"

"Sit." Shamus guided him to a metal folding chair.

Shamus wrapped a little more tape around Rogers's waist to secure him to the seat. He didn't expect resistance, and it was that much less to remove later.

"We need to talk, and then I need to go. But since you asked, I found you in the phone book, idiot!" What a loser!

* * *

Chang used his lights to part traffic and sped up 95 North. He took the exit for Shamus's complex and pulled around the corner from the entrance. He ignored the kids outside and entered the building.

The hallway was quiet. Chang found the apartment and knocked on the door but wasn't surprised when nobody answered. Chang looked over his shoulder and pulled out a thin pick. The lock was pure vanilla, and a minute later he stood inside. A whiff of gasoline hid under a stale, sour odor.

He drew his pistol and listened. Nothing at first, but the hair on the back of his neck rose. A mental image of scales sprouting down his back made him shiver. Something's here. He let the Dragon's ears search the empty space. He heard a drip, drip, drip, from a kitchen faucet and the faint buzz of a light tube.

The stench of gasoline grew more distinct and drew his gaze to the floor near the entrance. He picked out a ring-shaped stain. Gas can.

Chang tried to move silently toward the bedroom. His own feet made loud scraping noises on the cheap rug and worn boards, but it might've been his amplified hearing.

He cleared the bedroom and re-holstered his weapon. Nobody home. Half the hangers in the bedroom were empty. Packed light? Left in a hurry? All the dress shirts were wrapped in Sandy's Dry Cleaning bags. The white logo glowed in the dim room.

Chang walked toward the kitchen. The air felt thicker, and the fluorescent light reflected off the yellow walls gave the room a sickly cast. Left the light on for a reason?

Ribbons of odor snaked up his nostrils. Burnt cheese, old milk, lemons…

On the counter, Chang saw a vase that looked like something from a funeral home. It held dead roses, and a band of water clung to the bottom. Gray streaks wept down the sides.

He wrapped his handkerchief around his hand and opened the fridge. Mustard, a soda can, milk carton. Now the freezer.

His head snapped back from the face that glared at him. For an instant, he thought another head stared back, one with blazing eyes. Just a photo. Not even life-size, why did it… The cold fog brought a whiff of old death, and he turned his focus to the muddy sludge in the ice-cube trays. He sniffed more carefully. Bone, ash…and was that liniment oil? Same color as the streaks on the urn.

The scales rose on his neck again. Concentrate. He's gone. Where? Chang looked in the sink. Wet-paper smell. He reached in and scooped out a small wad. Nothing legible, but it might be from a magazine.

Where would Shamus go besides out of town? Not the dealership. His house? He thought of the night someone went through his trash. Was it Shamus? Guy couldn't be stupid enough to pick out another victim with them on his tail. Nelson was unlisted…wasn't he?

Chang looked at the phone book on the kitchen table. He pulled on a pair of latex gloves and felt the Dragon stare with him. He could see the bent corners of the pages past the middle. His heart began to pound. He thumbed through the Ps, the Qs, and reached the Rs. He flipped the pages faster, and his pulse jackhammered. A greasy thumbprint smudge right underneath Nelson's name…

Chang grabbed his cell.

* * *

"Are you going to ask what I want from you?"

"No."

Shamus was surprised. "Why not?"

"You're in control here. Have been since this whole thing started. If you want me to know, you'll tell me." Nelson sounded calm.

"True. I still am."

Nelson's phone chirped.

"I'll skip jokes about being tied up, but if you want me to answer that, it should be quick. It goes to voice mail soon," Nelson said, looking at Shamus.

Gotta be a trick, maybe to send a secret signal. "No. Let it go."

Nelson shrugged. The dog whined.

"How close were you to figuring it all out? How much does your partner and everyone else know?"

"Did you let the dog out?" Nelson gazed toward the front hall.

"What? Don't play with me. Tell me right now, or it's pain time." Shamus didn't like how this prey acted. He felt slippery.

"We're talking to car dealers. We still have to—"

Shamus grabbed a lighter and held the flame to Nelson's forearm. The guy screamed. "See? Don't jerk me around. I *know* you're close. *Exactly* how close? Do you want more?" Shamus waved the flame in front of the screamer's face.

Now the guy began to rock back and forth. What the hell was he doing? Was he chanting? "Stars on my arm, stars on my arm." Freak. Give him a shooting star to make a wish on…

Shamus touched the flame to the other arm. He could hear the guy suck air through his teeth. Now he was sweating like a horse. Shamus could see it pouring down his face. His fucking eyes wormed into Shamus's head.

"You're breaking down. All over your face. Ozone, fear, can't hold it in your body…" The weirdo sang out in a high-pitched, rhythmic cadence.

"Shut up!" Shamus backhanded Nelson, and the black eyes only got bigger. Like tar pits. Ouch! He let the lighter burn his own fingers. It flew out of his hand.

"Went too far…always screw up in the end…"

He smacked the other side of his face. Dark pools pulled his gaze back. Get control. Close the deal! He retrieved the lighter.

"Pick a number between one and ten; get it wrong and more fire, Scarecrow." Shamus searched for fear in the eyes. Nothing.

"One-two-three-four…four." Same high-pitched voice.

The eyes came from another world. Wouldn't let him go…picked through his mind.

"How…?" Nelson asked.

"Cats or rats before people? Cats." Not a question.

What the fuck? Shamus swung for his eye and landed on the cheek. His hand tingled.

"Wet the bed? Yesss."

"Shut up!" Swung and missed. He's in a chair!

"Scars all over. *All* over."

"Bullshit!" He can't see my legs.

"Deserved the punishment. Big disappointment…"

Who told him?

Nelson recoiled. Shamus knew it wasn't the beating. It felt like bugs were crawling in his brain. Lightheaded again.

"You were an *accident*…"

"How do you know?" Hurt his throat.

"They never wanted you…" Damn high voice cut right through Shamus's hands and into his ears.

"I'll *kill* you."

"Would anyway… Scared of girls…"

"Stop!"

"How they laughed…"

Shamus felt the floor rise up and hit him. Blood dripped on the floor. Not blood, tears. Snot ran down his nose, and he wiped it away with a sleeve.

Better now he couldn't see those eyes. Could still feel them.

"Let my dog go. All I want." More normal voice.

"Fine. First tell me. *How* close, stick man?" Hated the pleading tone.

"Too close, tick tock. Too close, tick tock." Again with the trance-voice.

Anger refreshed Shamus. Get a straight answer and get the fuck out of here.

"Okay." Shamus stumbled to the kitchen and found a knife. He returned to the hall and reached for the closet door. The dog whined and scratched at the wood.

"Wait!"

Now the guy sounded in the here and now.

Shamus held the knife and stood in front of Nelson. He avoided the penetrating gaze. "How'd you get on my trail?"

"Heather Cleary's body. Knew it was a car guy."

Shamus looked toward heaven. "See, Gran?"

Nelson's shirt was soaked through with sweat. The black lumps glittered. Should he cut his eyes out? No. Listen.

"How did you know so quickly?" Shamus didn't try to hide his curiosity.

"Puja."

"What the hell is puja?"

CHAPTER 54

On the Road Again

When Nelson didn't pick up the phone, it hit Chang how stupid he'd been. He imagined the sound of laughter from inside the freezer.

The wood staircase to the entrance shuddered when he pounded down two steps at a time. He hit the siren and lights. He was fifteen minutes away, easy.

He shot over to 95 South, but when he made it to the exit for Bear he saw an SUV crawl on the exit ramp. Chang almost lost control of the cruiser when he jammed on the brakes. He wondered if the driver was drunk, and then he saw the blond hair and silver cell phone against her ear. The huge vehicle weaved and blocked the entire ramp. Chang leaned on the horn and hit the siren, but she was oblivious.

He screamed a curse in Mandarin and stabbed the gas pedal. The impact with the back of the heavy vehicle knocked out the siren and left bits of grille on the road, but the driver *did* take the phone away from her ear.

She drifted left and stared with huge eyes at Chang when the cruiser drew past.

"Talk on your phone about *this!*" Chang sideswiped the SUV just to feel the impact. She braked and dropped the cell. He floored the accelerator, and the tires screeched.

Chang made it to Nelson's within minutes. He avoided the front of the house and pulled the car around back just out of sight of Nelson's windows.

He held up his shield to curious people in their back yards and put his finger to his lips. He took out a spare set of keys to Nelson's place and checked the set for one to the back doors. There was one for the upper door, but not for the sliding door on the ground floor.

He needed to come up from the basement to have a chance. No problem, the sliding glass door was simple enough. He had tools…

* * *

"Always wondered about those lemons. You got lucky." Shamus picked up the crowbar and rapped Nelson's scrawny shins. Careful. Don't break them.

The dog exploded with barks.

"We had a deal." Nelson squirmed in the chair.

"Who cares? You're about to be killed by that awful Hank Grant. He's in the other room." That got his attention.

"Hank's clumsy," Shamus continued. "Gonna bump his head just after he sets a fire to cover his tracks. Hank's going to burn your dog, not me."

"Cops won't buy that." He rocked nonstop.

"Only need a day, then I'm out of the country. Take 'em that long to sift through the ashes." Stay out of my mind!

"Dog can't turn you in! Let her out the back door and do what you have to. Kill me, but don't hurt my dog."

"Kill you? Thought you'd never ask..." Shamus picked up his backpack and rummaged through it. The dog barked and scratched at the door.

He heard a board creak from the basement stairs. The dog's bark became high-pitched and excited. Shamus looked up. Something was wrong.

"What was that?" He raised the revolver. The Ruger tumbled out of the backpack. He ignored it. He didn't like that sound. Now the dog made so much noise he couldn't hear anything else. Shamus walked toward the door that led to the basement.

Shamus heard a chair fall behind him. He whipped around. Crap! Somehow the skinny guy had worked free of the tape. Shamus thought of the Ruger nearby. That was stupid.

He aimed the revolver, but he saw Nelson dart to the hall closet and open the door. He rushed to follow.

"Daisy, attack!" Nelson shouted. The basset bounded out of the closet, leaped up, and licked his face.

The contrast between the command and the result of this pathetic attempt to escape brought a smile to his lips. He saw a nail clipper by the chair. Aha. Shamus heard a sound and turned back toward the basement door.

* * *

"Stop!" Chang pointed his .45 at the figure that moved toward Nelson and Daisy. His shot boomed into the wall when the target ducked at the last second and raced to the front hallway.

Chang heard Daisy bark and howl over his own ringing ears. He saw Nelson carry her through the swinging door to the kitchen. Shamus must be against the wall in the hallway.

A strange standoff. Chang could cover the door to the kitchen, but he didn't dare pop around the corner of the long front hallway. Shamus must see the kitchen door, but not Chang.

Where was he exactly? Listen... Chang breathed deeply and tuned the Dragon's ears to the hallway. He felt it strain for release. Not now...

"Drop your gun, cop, or I'll shoot them through the door!"

The guy's voice... Desperate... Chang used the sound to pinpoint where he stood in the hallway. He refused to acknowledge the face of the young Asian girl that floated in front of the wall. Can't hurt her now...

He took aim and fired the rest of his clip into the wall. The thin sheetrock would barely slow down the heavy caliber bullets. He ejected the magazine and slammed the second one home. He ran toward the hall, heard shots, and dove for a better angle.

* * *

Shamus felt three hard blows on his back. He fired several shots through the door to the kitchen. How did he punch me though the wall? His legs felt cold and wet. He sagged until he sat on the floor. Once he caught his breath, he'd run for the front door.

The kitchen door flew open, and Shamus saw several steel bowls crash against the wall. Nelson charged into the hallway and fell when he slipped on the rug, landing next to Shamus with a hard thump. Shamus wrapped his arm around his neck and pulled him close. The dog followed and barked.

* * *

Time slowed down for Chang, and he viewed the hallway through the Dragon's eyes. He held the gun in both hands. He saw movement, heard a metallic clatter, then a shout. He fired at a blur of a figure. Just when he pulled the trigger, the guy dropped. Missed! Chang saw Nelson sprawled on the hall floor, the runner carpet bunched by his feet where he'd slipped. Nelson held a paring knife, and steel nesting bowls surrounded him. His face was bruised and swollen. Shamus had grabbed Nelson and pulled him too close for Chang to risk a shot.

Chang could see three blood streaks down the wall and rose-shaped blotches on the white painter's outfit. Even so, Shamus managed to stand and keep the revolver pressed against Nelson's head. Daisy's barks pounded Chang's skull.

Chang crept down the hallway, his weapon trained on Shamus.

"Back off!" Shamus's voice carried a raspy, wet quality, but he was steady on his feet. He reached back and turned the knob to the front door.

"Let him go. You need an ambulance."

"Fuck you." Shamus opened the door and backed up. Daisy bolted for the daylight, and the two men tripped over her long body.

"Daisy, no!" Nelson groped for the dog and tried to crawl after her. Shamus held onto the pistol and grabbed the back of Nelson's shirt.

Chang closed the distance. One more step and he could kick the gun away. Paramedics still might pull him through… Chang stopped short. Shamus struggled to pull

Nelson toward him and looked back. Chang gazed with his own eyes at Shamus, then shot him twice in the face.

CHAPTER 55

No Harm, No Foul

Dover, Monday

Despite the cool spring day, Chang's uniform felt itchy. The ceremony dragged on, and he barely remembered the reporters' questions afterward. Byrd's huge grin and shiny head danced in his mind. Nancy Brand's sharp outfit and strawberry-shampoo scent stayed with him, too. Was she just being nice when she whispered, "Want your clothes back?"

He tucked the commendation award under his arm and took the stairs up to his desk. The governor had piled on praise, maybe even meant it. Then again, she was all smiles with Byrd in front of the cameras.

He stayed as long as required, said his lines as per instruction, and climbed Shu's mountains while the flashbulbs recorded his empty smiles. Nelson, bruises and all, was just another face in the crowd during the ceremony. Chang scratched his neck under the tight collar and put the commendation on his desk.

When he saw the light go on in Byrd's office, he walked over. Didn't bother to knock. Byrd looked up and registered annoyance for a moment. His decoration-covered chest and polished boots gleamed. Several copies of the *Daily Post* sat on his desk. Chang saw the headline: “Killer Deal.”

“Ah, the star of the show. Sit down.”

“No thanks.”

Byrd shrugged.

“Chang, you did the right thing out there for everyone. Maybe you can be a good soldier after all. I’ll need help next year and after that when I win.”

“I’m sure, sir.”

“You should be happy. You got your man, a clean report on the shoot, and the lab work already backs your case. Somehow, you got to be the big hero after all.”

“Not somehow, sir.” Would it kill him to mention Nelson’s name?

Byrd lowered his voice. “Chang, I know what was going on. I’m not stupid, you know.”

“Confucius say: Smartest man in room, sometimes stand alone.”

Byrd’s face turned brick-red.

“I should have known better. You’ve saved yourself, but your badge was on the line. Don’t risk it by embarrassing the department. Got it?” Byrd’s bushy eyebrows formed a single furry line across his forehead.

“Why don’t you keep it safe for me?” Chang flipped his shield on Byrd’s desk and drew his service weapon. He savored the flicker of fear in Byrd’s eyes.

Chang removed the magazine and racked the slide to eject the chambered round. It landed on top of a newspaper and rolled to the floor.

Byrd said something, but Chang skied down the snowy slopes of Mount Shu and couldn’t hear him.

* * *

Chang left his uniform in the locker room and walked to Nelson's cubicle in his civvies. Nelson's bruises were already fading. Even better, Chang saw no signs Nelson was going to hibernate inside his own mind.

"You made it official?" Chang felt tension drop from his shoulders.

"I left a letter. My boss is a good guy, and I don't do drama."

Chang watched Nelson take out a pen and scribble "Nelson wuz here" on his desk.

EPILOGUE

Four weeks later

Chang tried to be quiet while he searched Nancy's kitchen for a mug. He grabbed the kettle before it shrieked. She hadn't woken up when he'd gotten out of bed, and he wanted to let her sleep.

He slipped out the front door to retrieve the morning paper. Pink light tinged the dark sky. Inside, he turned to the opinion page to see if the rumor about Patrick Flannigan was true. Chang thought the grainy picture with the byline had to have been retouched. Those teeth hadn't been white in decades.

Off to Grayer Pastures
By Patrick Flannigan

We once thought our career would end not with a bang but a whimper here in the gentle bosom of Wilmington. Fate's fickle hand had other ideas, and we head once again for points north and return to the New York Times.

With the conclusion of the Iceman case, we leave for one last dance with the Old Gray Lady. We wish the people of Wilmington well and thank them for their years of support. We know they will sleep soundly for two reasons. First, the one-man reign of terror that was Shamus Ryan has come to an end. Second, that Delawareans will no longer have to rely on the callous good fortune of detectives like Paul Chang. His "heroics" came at the potential cost of his own friend's life when he dangled the poor fellow as bait. The force is well rid of such renegades.

Ironically, the self-styled Iceman himself was more forthcoming than the state police. We hope the experience inspires a new approach, one that trusts the people with information.

So, we pen this column with mixed emotions. We leave the Daily Post *in younger and more capable hands and look forward to a return to New York. To Wilmington, a fond farewell. To Chang and the rest of the stonewallers, good riddance.*

Finally, a point of agreement. Shu was better at ignoring such taunts, but at least the bitter old man would be out of his life.

"You're up early."

Chang turned and saw Nancy propped up in the doorway. She was wearing his shirt again. He gazed at her bare legs. "Maybe you should keep that." A nice surprise last night.

"After you ripped half the buttons off?"

Such a cute smile. "Bill me." He fought off the urge for a repeat performance.

Nancy looked more serious. "You were awake when I dozed off last night. Didn't you get any sleep?"

"I have a lot to do today." Chang hoped she wouldn't force him to lie about staying up all night.

Her pause told him she caught the dodge. "I understand."

No, she didn't. Maybe if they lasted a while he'd explain about the Nightmare. Chang picked up the manila envelope from the kitchen table. "I guess I'm legal now."

"Ready to hang out the proverbial shingle. I made sure they spelled everything right."

She'd also cleared the last of Byrd's bureaucratic roadblocks at the licensing office.

"Thanks," Chang said.

"Just trying to buy a vote for my boss."

"For last night..."

Her kiss made him forget all about the Flannigan piece.

* * *

"What do you think?" Chang held up the framed license for East-West Investigations. The smell of fresh paint and new carpet hung in the air.

"Who'd you sleep with to get that approved so fast?" Nelson grinned.

He was out of his shell today.

"I'm a gentleman." State police controlled the approvals, but Nancy knew Byrd didn't need any bad press in an election year.

"Dried seahorse?" Nelson sounded like a new man. Chang wasn't sure if he liked it or not.

"A few dinners and your imagination runs wild." Chang lowered his voice. "Seahorse not needed, thank you very much." No mystery to his own good mood.

"Any chance she'll get to dine at Shu's House of Mandarin Delight soon?"

"Thirsty man who find well, not share with Dragon Queen."

"That's a no?"

"You're going to make an excellent gumshoe."

* * *

Chang and Nelson greeted Shu when he opened the front door. The incense burned, but tonight it was a light, flowery fragrance. It was late for Nelson, nearly eleven o'clock, but Chang hoped his mother would still be alert. For her this was early.

They waited while Shu assisted her to the parlor. Chang understood. Too proud to see guests in her bedroom.

"Paul finally come when he knows I better." Tai Kai waved the two into the room. Shu drifted out. Chang held his tongue. Even with the new lease and efforts to set up the new office, he visited every night. Her last bout of pain scared even Shu, but either he or the doctors had done something right.

"You look good tonight, Mother."

"What you know?"

Chang wanted to say he had great taste in women, but he knew that would bring up another round of Colleen-bashing.

He explained about the new private investigation firm he was starting with Nelson. He resorted to Mandarin when she didn't understand. She wrinkled her nose when he did. He told her the name. She closed her eyes and then looked at Chang.

"It suit you."

Tai Kai turned toward Nelson. "You fired, too?"

"No, ma'am. I resigned. Computers are too boring."

"Safe, not boring. You quit to work with Paul?"

"Yes, ma'am."

"Maybe you crazy again." She paused and pointed at Chang. "When he look for rat, you watch out for tiger."

* * *

"If we hurry, we can catch last call at Tea Hee." Chang sped up before he remembered he didn't have his get-out-of-jail-free card anymore.

Even so, they reached the shop, and to his surprise it was crowded with young folks. He watched Nelson look at the drink specials and all the elaborate blends. Chang ordered some hot water for his ginseng.

"Who's next?"

"I am." Nelson sounded confident. "I'll have a tall 'Chai of the Tiger' please, for here." He smiled at Chang. "Appropriate, don't you think?"

"Sorry. We're all out of the 'Tiger.' Can I get you something else?" The line grew behind them. One kid looked at his watch.

Nelson didn't miss a beat. "Certainly. I'll have the Earl Grey."

ABOUT THE AUTHOR

J. Gregory Smith was born and raised in Washington, DC. He earned his Bachelor of Arts in English from Skidmore College, and his Master's in Business Administration from the College of William & Mary. A public relations professional in DC, Smith continued his work after moving to Delaware. He now writes full time.